WILD WITHIN

WILD AT HEART SERIES, BOOK ONE

BY CHRISTINE HARTMANN

WILD WITHIN

Limitless Publishing, LLC
Kailua, HI 96734
www.limitlesspublishing.com

Formatting: Limitless Publishing

ISBN-13: 978-1-68058-419-6
ISBN-10: 1-68058-419-7

DEDICATION

For Ron, my Mr. Romantic.

CHAPTER 1

Early morning sun scorched the grimy car hood and forced its way through the window to burn Grace's bare arms. She fidgeted as she watched the arid plane of sagebrush and light brown dust roll past. The landscape differed completely from the grassy hills, eucalyptus trees, and fog around her native San Francisco. Occasional yucca plants shouldered their way between low scraggly bushes with more branches than leaves. Small boulders peppered the area, looking like enormous grey cottage cheese curds among rolling, sere hills.

This countryside puts the wild in wilderness.

The car bounced past dry pastures and scruffy woods.

Maybe I should have spent more time reading those trail guides?

A glimpse of the Mexican border made her sit up straight.

Who cares? I'm here.

Grace bounced in her seat with excitement.

This is it.

Grace and her friend Celine were the only people at the five square wooden posts that marked the southern terminus of the 2,665-mile Pacific Crest Trail, a route leading from Mexico to Canada. A few yards away, wind forced its way through the steel border fence like the sound of screeching tires. Celine snapped a few pictures as Grace removed the spiral hiker register from its protective metal box. On the first empty page she wrote:

Kenji, you're with me.

She signed with more bravado than she actually felt.

Grace spurted back to the car. "I want to get going." But her backpack, resting in the backseat, was in less of a hurry. She coaxed it onto her shoulders with much grunting and straining and stood, slightly bent, for one final snapshot.

"I've never lifted anything this heavy. What was I thinking? It's not a trip to Macy's where I can throw all the heavy stuff into the trunk."

"You were thinking you might need some supplies." Celine surveyed her. "Because you're going to be in the middle of nowhere. For months."

"Thanks for the reminder." Grace straightened with effort. "I've been waiting almost a year for this. They say your pack gets lighter as you get used to it. So where's the trail?"

Celine shrugged. Grace searched the monotonous sand and brush.

"I've got the map on my cell."

But the phone wouldn't turn on. Grace depressed

the controls repeatedly. The screen remained as black as its case.

Come on. My paper maps are buried in my pack.

She took a mental inventory of what lay above them: a one-person tent, a sleeping bag and mat, a wide-brimmed sun hat, extra socks, the head of a toothbrush, all-weather matches, a travel-size deodorant stick, her mother's homemade rice cakes, and Kenji's apartment key fastened with a twist tie to the zipper of a first aid kit. The idea of spreading everything out at the base of the monument made her ill.

She pushed more buttons.

Don't die now.

The screen flickered. She fiddled more and the contrast increased.

"Typical me." Her hands shook a little as she pinched the trail map to zoom in on her location. "I turned down the brightness last night to save energy. For a second there, I thought I was going to faint. That would've made a good Facebook post. Grace Mori's one second thru-hike of the PCT."

Celine grinned and poked Grace's arm. "It's good to get all the mistakes out of the way at the beginning. Now try to make it through the rest of the day without any more."

Grace stepped into the sparse brush.

"I already miss you as much as I miss your brother," Celine called after her. But the wind whipped away her words.

On the trail, Grace's pent up excitement gave wings to her hiking shoes. They floated across baked earth that meandered through scrub and around boulders. She raced securely down descents and sailed up ascents.

This is so easy.

She covered the next two miles in under an hour. Her initial destination was Lake Morena County Park, eighteen miles away. But her thoughts were of the Canadian border.

Twenty miles a day, for the next four months, before the northern mountains become impassable with snow. In this heat, that idea feels like a mirage.

She looked at her watch.

Nine thirty. Ten more hours of daylight. So I'll get to Lake Morena with time to spare.

At first, the white circle rising in a cloudless blue seemed a happy part of the scenery. But bit by bit, the sun blazed an ever fiercer hole in the sky. Her short black hair melted into her head and burned her fingers when she touched it.

I should never have given up lightening my hair. Apparently blondes do have more fun, even in the desert.

Her legs pistoned in long strides that searched for cover. But nothing afforded shade.

A tree. A bush. A houseplant, for goodness sake. I'll take anything.

The trail eventually crossed a highway and meandered through a grove of cottonwood trees. There, Grace slung off her pack, dropped beside it, and dug through her gear.

She squashed a cream-colored hat onto her sweaty brow. Her parched lips drained a water bottle. A rough trunk supported her back.

My shoulders ache. My feet hurt. And this pack

4

weighs a ton. Why did I throw in everything I thought might come in handy? Pre-moistened body wipes? Am I really going to need those out here?

The previous night, she and Celine had discussed her strategy. "I read somewhere a person hiking in direct sun needs at least a gallon of water for every ten miles." Grace laid out her water containers on the hotel bed. "But one gallon weighs eight pounds. I've got a two-gallon collapsible water container and two one-liter bottles. Do you think I should fill them all? That's close to twenty extra pounds."

"I think you should follow the rules."

"That's a lot of extra weight." Grace hefted a container from the hotel sink. "Maybe I'll fill two bottles and leave my larger container partially empty. I'll drink a lot before I start. And Hauser Creek is on the trail. I can get more water there."

Celine pursed her lips contemplatively and tossed an empty bottle to Grace. "What if there's no water in the creek?"

"Then they wouldn't call it a creek." Grace chucked the bottle back at her. "It'll be fine. Like I said, I'll hydrate like crazy before we set out."

In the morning, after a brief rest under cottonwoods, Grace continued her hike. She chased lazy clouds in search of shade. They vaporized before she reached them.

Why did I wear pants?

She longed for the hiking skirt in her pack. Then the trail narrowed, and waist-high chaparral brush clung and tore as she battled through. Rough, aggressive limbs and thick, unforgiving leaves pulled at her hiking poles. Grace held them above her head, unable to see her feet. After five minutes of struggle, she reached the other side. Her face dripped with sweat. She looked down.

I love you, pants.

Grace drained her second water bottle as she climbed. At the top of the hill, she paused. Perspiration dripped into her eyes and mouth, but she was too hot to care. In the distance, the border wall and Mexican mountains were still clearly visible. She thought of fishing out her phone for a picture.

Too much effort.

The path leveled out. Her pace slowed. The heat irritated her.

I should have had my hat on from the beginning. Why didn't I start hiking earlier in the day? Where the heck is Hauser Creek? I need more water.

She wiped a hot tear from her cheek.

What a mess. But there's no point in crying. Come on Grace.

Grace was the kind of person who prided herself on being someone people could count on. When her mother's first attempt at baked Alaska set the kitchen window curtains aflame, teenage Grace doused the inferno in chocolate syrup, then helped her mother take down the gooey mess.

"People in Alaska originally lived in igloos. They probably didn't have window curtains." She wiped the counter with a Lysol-soaked dishrag. "Some desserts don't translate well across climate zones."

As an adult, Grace volunteered her services as a psychologist for the Friday overnight shift at the

Berkeley women's crisis hotline. There, she comforted agonized rape victims, beaten girlfriends, and conflicted housewives with a sympathetic ear, sensible advice, and a list of referrals she'd personally vetted.

"You're ready to move out? Don't forget to take his Rolex. He owes you big time."

And when tragedy struck her family a year ago, it was Grace who negotiated with the funeral home and the florist. Phoned relatives in San Diego, New Brunswick, and Tokyo. Late at night, in bed alone, she lay exhausted but sleepless.

"How am I going to get through this by myself?"

That blistering day on the trail, she began to lose faith. The merciless, prodding sun became her enemy. It evaporated her enthusiasm, diminished her stamina, and gnawed at her judgment. Her feet dragged along the sandy path without any of their initial eagerness. She refilled her water bottles from the large container in her pack and ignored the voice that told her she would soon run out of fluids.

After another mile, the trail merged with a Jeep road. In the distance, Grace saw a disappearing cloud of dust.

That was a car. I could have asked them for a ride. Maybe they had air conditioning. Some extra water. Maybe they were on their way back to San Diego and would have taken me to a hotel. I could have started the trail again in a few days, when it's cooler.

She checked the phone's GPS. Four miles to Hauser Creek.

I'll make it if I ration my water.

By the time the trail dove into Hauser Canyon's shaded grove of oaks and sycamores, Grace hated the sun more than she'd ever hated anything. She squinted at the wooded valley. But the only hint that a creek had ever flowed across the parched land was a strip of slightly darker sand meandering through a pile of rocks. Grace's knees wobbled.

Even in the shade, sweat poured down her face.

It's past noon. I should eat.

She felt nauseous. Her head pulsed like molten lava in a live volcano crater.

I need to rest.

Her shoulders shrugged out of the pack straps and she sank to the ground. Before thinking better of it, she drank the rest of her water. A small Japanese folding fan, the parting gift from her sister, offered some relief. The hot desert air drew out the fan's sandalwood scent. The breeze evaporated her perspiration.

She kicked off her shoes and socks, then changed into her skirt. But after thirty minutes of inertia, sweat still dripped from her chin. Sitting made her dizzy, so she lay down. The violent sun tortured her through the leaves, shafts branding her face and body like flames.

I need more water. Have to keep going. A road's not far ahead. If I lie down in the middle, somebody will find me.

But the idea of crawling out of the partial shade into the glaring sun was too much.

Bees droned near her head.

What's that? Airplane? Maybe they can see me down here. Call in a rescue.

Her mind drifted up, into the sparse tree branches. It hung there briefly. Then ascended into the smoldering, cloudless sky.

Later, another idea broke through her confusion.

I'm going to die. On my first day on the trail. Kind of a waste. All this equipment. All that money. Geez, I could have spent it on those cell phone-operated blinds for the living room instead. There was that coupon in the Saturday clipper magazine...

Her tongue ran along dry lips.

Hmm. I'm licking a lizard. I wonder if he'll lick back.

Then Grace thought of nothing.

CHAPTER 2

Cool water.

It drenched her hair and flowed into her brown eyes. It dripped off her stubby nose and splashed against her mouth.

"Hey." The voice called from far away. "Hey, wake up."

Grace ignored it, preoccupied with the water. She opened her lips and some trickled in.

Yummy.

She opened her mouth wider and gulped. Liquid clogged her windpipe. She choked and turned her head, sputtering and gagging.

"Easy now." The voice had a soft drawl. "I'm giving you a little shower."

More liquid dribbled over her head.

Delightful.

"It's hot as the hinges of hell out here. And I find you taking a siesta. In this kind of situation, somebody might think you're trying to kill yourself. Except for the huge pack, of course. That kind of gives away this was an accident."

"What?" Grace wiped her eyes and blinked in the sun.

"I was saying, next time you should be more careful. If you don't take enough water into the desert, chances are pretty good you'll never come out."

"What?"

The man laughed in an attractive, radio announcer bass. "Here, sit up a bit so you can drink. This isn't nap time. You've still got some hiking to do."

Grace looked around. A broad face with reddish stubble on a youthful chin grinned down at her. The man had a bandana tied around his neck. The bright blue matched his clear eyes.

Grace pushed herself onto her elbows. "Who are you?"

"Name's Lone Star. Pleased to meet you…?" He reached out his hand.

"Grace. Grace Mori." She winced as he enfolded her hand in a tight, deep grip.

"Just Grace? No trail name?"

"No what?"

"Trail name. Out here on the trail—which is where you are and where you're going to stay if I have anything to do with it—we've got trail names. People don't use real names too much. But suit yourself, Just Grace. Now, let's see how you're doing."

Lone Star felt her forehead with the back of his freckled hand. "No fever. That's good. Let's see what some more hydration will do."

He handed Grace a three-liter Coke bottle filled

11

with water. Two rows of sparkling teeth shone in his handsome, tanned face. "Drink all you want, darlin'. I was a scout. I come prepared." He patted the bright yellow backpack behind him. "Got more where that came from."

Grace guzzled the water.

"Whoa, there. Not all in one gulp. Let's take it one step at a time, okay?"

In the next thirty minutes, Grace finished half the bottle. The sun still beat through the trees, but she stopped sweating. Her head hurt less than before. When she felt steady enough to stand, she had the sudden urge to relieve herself.

"That's a good sign." Lone Star clapped his hand on her shoulder. Grace's face flushed. He chuckled. "You're totally green, aren't you? Well, the way it works on the trail is you go pee anywhere you want. I won't look."

Grace pulled on socks and stuffed aching feet into low-top boots. The trail led her past a clearing in the trees. Lone Star called after her. "Take a look and see what color it is."

Grace turned. "Excuse me?"

"If your pee is brown, we're not out of the woods yet." He gestured at their surroundings, grinning at his double-entendre. "If your pee's close to the color of my pack, I'd say you're safe to start hiking again, okay?"

When Grace returned, Lone Star raised his eyebrows. She tapped his yellow pack with one finger. He smiled and cupped his hands.

"Whoo-hah! Let's get this show on the road." He donned enormous hiking shoes and hoisted his pack across his bulky shoulders with ease. "The sun's angle tells me we've got plenty of time to get to Lake Morena." Grace reached for her pack straps, but Lone Star restrained her. "Not so fast, little lady."

"You want me to leave this here? I spent months putting it all together. I can't abandon it."

"No, ma'am. I want you to hike another six miles today. We have to get you to a cool place and a water resupply."

"But then…"

Lone Star swung her pack onto his chest. His arms looped through the straps backward. He adjusted the pack to ride high, under his chin.

Grace's mouth hung open. "You're going to carry both."

Lone Star flexed his muscular arms. Grace stared at the biceps that strained the material of his shirt.

"Nothing like a little exercise." He bowed and swept his arm across the two-foot-wide trail. "After you."

The path ascended steeply. Lone Star let Grace set the pace and maintained a constant stream of banter from behind. He drew her attention to rock formations and different types of plant life, to field mice sunning themselves on stones and falcons drifting lazily on thermals.

"Stop me if I'm boring you. I know I can talk the needles off a cactus."

"You're not boring. You're distracting. In this heat, I can use it."

Nothing changed about the landscape, but to Grace the desert felt softer. Her pulse quickened.

Her hands warmed. She relaxed more than she had been able to in years. For the first time, she noticed the chaparral's sage scent. Subtle color differences in surrounding hills and flatland stood out more clearly. Even the sun seemed gentler.

This stranger didn't probe into her personal life, but Grace gradually revealed things she'd never told anyone. About the time her skirt caught on her junior high school locker door and fell around her ankles as the boy's gym line walked past. About her two-bedroom condominium in San Rafael, California. And about Kenji.

CHAPTER 3

A year earlier, in mid-April, Grace returned home for the annual Mori Family Cherry Blossom Viewing Picnic. The backyard cherry tree branches quivered with pink blossoms. Fallen petals speckled a grey bedspread laid for a picnic. A gentle breeze ruffled the pale green grass. Scents of blooming roses and grilled fish floated on the light breeze, filling Grace's mind with childhood memories.

Her brother, Kenji, ran barefoot across the lawn toward her. Purple Lakers basketball shorts flapped around his skinny legs. A tattered, black '*I love my Harley'* t-shirt billowed out behind him.

He gave Grace a bear hug. "It's great to see you."

Grace tugged on his shirt. "I see you dressed up for the occasion."

"Dressed down is the new dressed up."

"Where's Hope?"

"You know our sister. She's inside helping Mom cook."

Kenji glanced toward the house, where a slender

African American woman in her early twenties had just shut the back door. Her approach over the lawn was slow and deliberate. A defiant look clouded her face, contrasting with the breezy white tunic she wore over a lacy pink camisole.

"Celine, don't look so serious." Kenji grabbed her outstretched hand and pulled her close by his side. "This is Grace, my oldest sister."

Celine gave a forced smile.

Grace laughed. "I know that look. You feel like you've walked into a scene from *Guess Who's Coming to Dinner*, right? Only our mom's no Katharine Hepburn. And Dad's no Japanese Gary Cooper."

Celine's frown didn't budge. "Spencer Tracy."

"Right."

"He was an ass in that movie."

"Well, our mom and dad can be that too. But they're essentially harmless. Seriously. Watch this. This is how Mom looked, right?" Grace stepped back and surveyed the young couple, hands on hips, eyes narrowed, lips stretched into a thin, lopsided sneer.

The corners of Celine's mouth turned up. "I think your mom wanted to shoot me. You don't have a gun in the house, do you?"

"It's not personal." Kenji wrapped his arm around Celine's slim waist. "She always hates my girlfriends. Has, ever since high school."

Grace pushed an errant wave of Kenji's hair back from his face. "To have Kenji invite you to the annual Mori Cherry Blossom Viewing Picnic is a big deal. It means he's serious. That scares our

16

mom."

Kenji kissed Celine's hand. "Between us, Grace, Celine and I *are* serious. After my hike this summer, Celine and I are making plans."

Celine smiled at Grace. But her eyes warned of a firmness that would be dangerous to test.

Mrs. Mori appeared at the back door. She stared at the conclave and then at her watch.

"That's a hint." Kenji led the way across the lawn and into the house.

Later, after the picnic, the family sat among empty beer bottles under the cherry tree. Hope's children lay stretched on their stomachs, feet kicking absently at the grass.

Hope stroked her daughter's hair and looked at Grace. "We're going to give the twins separate bedrooms this summer. They're getting too old to share a room. But I'm worried about how they'll react. Do you remember how upset you were when Mom gave me my own bedroom?"

"I wasn't upset because you were moving *out*, if that's what you mean. I was upset because Kenji was moving *in*. You're the one who got a room to yourself. I'm the one who had to switch to the bottom bunk and have my little brother throw toy train engines and Lego airplanes at me all night."

"It wasn't my idea. Mom knew you'd be a better influence on him than I was. Remember that pink bed and desk set she bought me for the new room? She thought she could turn me into a Japanese version of Barbie."

"And you proved her wrong by plastering the walls with heavy metal band stickers."

"I had to rebel."

"And you're prepared for these two to do that when you split them up, right?" Grace glanced at her niece and nephew, who'd fallen asleep. "I can't believe they're eight already."

"Eight going on fifteen. They've started conversing in a secret language, like we did. But theirs is incomprehensible."

"I think ours was too, at least to Mom. She didn't learn a lot of Pig Latin in those Tuesday night English conversation classes."

"It's like they're in their own world when they're together." Hope sighed. "Maybe we shouldn't split them up after all."

"Why don't you leave two beds in one of the rooms and see what happens? I bet they'll like having their own space, and if they feel like they've got the option of being together, it won't feel so scary or forced. Sometimes you have to give things time."

"I guess that's why you're the psychologist. What's the bill?"

"Sisterly rate. Look for it in the mail."

"Thanks for thinking outside the box. And now I think these two need a nap in your old bunk bed." Hope shook her children awake and ushered them inside.

A minute later, Kenji sauntered across the grass toward the back door. Mrs. Mori followed, carrying a pile of dirty dishes. Kenji reached for the plates. But his mother didn't let go. A small pulling match ensued. Grace chuckled.

But then Kenji's face clouded with anger. He

raised his voice. Everyone under the tree strained to hear.

Mrs. Mori shook a finger at him.

Phrases wafted across the lawn. "It's none of your business. You can't control my goddamned life. I'm sick of this. Give it up, Mom."

Kenji shoved the stack of plates and his mother fell into the railing. The clatter of smashing stoneware reverberated in the evening stillness. People on the blanket rushed toward the house. Grace took the stairs two at a time and reached Kenji first. She pulled him inside. Celine followed. Mr. Mori stayed with his wife, his stage whispered Japanese reaching down the hallway.

"Ungrateful…inexcusable…I will talk with him."

Inside, Kenji tore from Grace's grip, stomped into the living room, and snatched a motorcycle helmet from among the potted orchids. Celine walked up to him and, without saying a word, rested her hand on his forearm. He deposited the helmet on the sofa. She pulled him to her, stroked his head, and whispered into his ear. Grace watched for a moment from the hall and then slipped into the bathroom.

I'll give Mom and Dad a few minutes before trying to make peace.

She straightened the shower curtains and refolded a guest towel that had fallen to the floor. A door slammed in the distance.

What a way to introduce Celine to the family, poor girl. No wonder I never bring anybody home.

A quiet knock startled her.

"Grace? Can I come in?"

Grace opened the door to Celine.

Grace stepped aside. "I'll give you some privacy."

"No. Let me come in. If it's okay." Celine's bright face showed evidence of tears. "I have to clean up a bit." She lifted a red leather clutch.

Grace sat on the bathtub rim.

Celine rubbed her cheeks with a tissue. "Kenji went home."

"Didn't you two come together?"

"He goes everywhere on that motorcycle. I took my car and met him here. I'll go in a second. But I thought I should say goodbye to your parents first. No sense making a bad impression." She paused to apply mauve lipstick. "Well, it's probably too late for that. They won't forget *me* easily. This wasn't exactly what Kenji and I had in mind when we planned this introduction to your family. But I'm an adult, and I want to act like one. Whatever your parents think, my mama didn't raise me up to be a guest who doesn't thank her hosts." She snapped the blush container closed.

"Politeness is obviously something you don't have in common with Kenji."

"You should see him outside of this house more." Celine glanced into the mirror to check her face. "I don't mean that you two don't see enough of each other. I mean he's good with people. Normally. I bet he learned it from you."

Grace's fingers played with the shower curtain. "I'm not so sure about that."

"That's not what Kenji says." Celine put eyeliner

20

and mascara back in her bag. "I'm ready." She smiled. "Let's face the music."

Half an hour later, Grace leaned against the front door and gazed into the suburban night. Lamps from the enormous house across the street illuminated the narrow front lawn. A mockingbird called like a crosswalk chirp. In the distance sirens wailed, the sound drifting on what was left of the earlier breeze. Inside, the house was quiet. An occasional clinking of dishes floated down the hall.

The telephone's shrill chime disturbed the silence. Grace turned. Mrs. Mori shuffled from the kitchen in slippers and picked up the hallway receiver.

"Hello." Fatigue accentuated her Japanese accent. "Mori residence…yes."

And something in the tone of her voice made Grace step away from the door. Mrs. Mori slumped against the wall. Grace broke into a run. The receiver clattered to the floor and skidded toward the kitchen.

Grace caught her mother as she collapsed.

"Kenji. My baby…"

***

Earlier, Celine had left the Mori home and driven along the main route out of town, where she encountered police officers setting up reflective cones.

She rolled down the window to talk to an officer.

"You can't go this way, I'm afraid." A tall Latino officer raised his hand. "There's been an accident. We're setting up a detour. But if you know the roads, you can probably turn around before it gets too crowded. You'd better hurry though."

People had come out of their houses. Some walked down their driveways, ushering children in Spiderman and Thomas the Train pajamas toward the street.

Celine grated the car's gears to put it into quick reverse. As she swung around, her high beams revealed two parked police cars with their headlights pointed at the base of a telephone pole. Several officers bent over a motorcycle. She slammed the car into park, threw open the door, and raced toward the bike.

"No!"

The officers held out their arms in appeal. She ignored them.

A well-cushioned older man in uniform scooped her up and held her gently under the armpits. "Ma'am, you have to go back to your car."

Celine's legs strained against the pavement.

"Ma'am, there's nothing for you to see here."

Afterward, Celine said she didn't remember anything but the motorcycle. A massive silver body glowing in the bright light. Front wheel and fork bent ninety degrees. Unscathed leather saddlebags, with silver studs that glittered like diamonds, spelling out the Japanese symbol for peace.

Celine said she didn't remember the officers identifying her as the girlfriend of the crash victim. Or their leading her to a squad car. She didn't recall the ambulance arriving with a wailing siren. Or its leaving in silence.

At some point, she fished out her cell phone.

"I have to call his parents. Somebody's got to tell them."

A female officer cupped her hand gently around Celine's trembling fingers. "We'll do that for you if you'd like. We'll send somebody out to the house."

"No. They should hear it from somebody they know." But after choking out, "Mrs. Mori? It's Celine. Kenji…there was an accident," all she could do was sob.

CHAPTER 4

When Grace finished the story, Lone Star stepped softly to her side.

"Hey, Just Grace. Let's stop here for a sec." He lifted her chin and tried to catch her evasive eyes. "That story breaks my heart. I've got four brothers and two sisters. If anything happened to them, I think I'd open myself up a worm farm."

Grace lifted her gaze. "A what?"

"A cemetery. I mean, I assume…" Lone Star scuffed a deep line in the dirt with the toe of his shoe.

"He died."

"Yeah." He rubbed his heel across the trench, erasing it. "That's what I'd feel like doing if anything happened to someone in my family."

"I know." Grace walked slowly on. "You're right. You do. I mean, I think part of me did die with him. At least, life hasn't seemed the same since."

Lone Star strode in front and blocked the path. Grace focused on his sparkling blue eyes. They shone with the sunlight and something else, something both soothing and energizing. Eventually, she turned away and sighed. "It's just not the easiest to talk about. Today of all days."

"You mean…"

"It happened a year ago."

"Today?"

"Today."

"Miss Grace Mori." Lone Star wrapped her hands in his. "I'm truly sorry."

Two tears ran down Grace's dusty cheeks, leaving shimmering tracks. Lone Star lowered her pack and pulled her to him. She leaned her head against his chest and wept. Large hands stroked her erratically heaving back. Her arms extended slack at her side and then, after a while, reached up and pulled him to her. She buried her face deeper into his shoulder.

No one has held me like this since it happened.

When her tears diminished, Lone Star pushed her gently from him. "I know you must feel lower than a gopher hole right about now. But I'm worried about your expelling all that salt. We've still got a ways to go."

Grace wiped her eyes with her sleeve. "I need a salt lick, like they put out for deer."

Lone Star's eyes twinkled. "Good idea. Have some more water for now. Then we'll set about finding you one."

Grace's mouth stretched into a brief grin. Lone Star handed her the big water bottle. She gulped, burped, and turned bright red.

"Excuse me." She handed the bottle back to him.

"Do you feel a little better?"

"Yes. I think that cry had been building up for a year. Sorry you got caught in the flood."

Lone Star wiped the large water mark on his shirt with exaggerated swipes of his bandana. "Not to worry. It's quick-dry."

He watched Grace stride ahead and wiped his forehead with his bandana. "That's one heck of a woman." He marched after her. "I think it's my turn to tell a story, Just Grace. What do you want to know about me?"

She answered without turning around. "Something less dramatic than what I just told you. Let's start with what you do."

"You mean when I'm not rescuing ladies in distress?"

"What's your day job?"

"I'm an education attorney. We represent private and public educational institutions, but I work mostly with school districts."

"That seems like a niche market for an attorney."

Lone Star readjusted Grace's pack on his chest. "Coming up, my one goal was to be a lawyer. Don't ask me why. I must have seen a lawyer do something great on TV once. I used to watch a lot of TV. But then I found out you need money to go to law school. My family didn't exactly ride high on the hog. So I figured I would never go."

Grace turned to look at him. "But you're a lawyer now. What happened?"

"A dust storm."

"Huh?"

"I'm from El Paso. West Texas. We have a lot of

dust storms. Ever seen one?"

"No."

"Well, it's like a tsunami of dust rising all the way to the sky. Like a flowing wall that goes from the clouds clear down to the ground." Lone Star's hands waved across the horizon. "When it sweeps through, you can have outages, property damage, crop damage, a long list of trouble. When I was in eighth grade, we had a fierce one, so fierce it took down all the power lines. Didn't get power back for a week. That's what saved me."

Grace shook her head. "I don't get it."

"No power. No TV. And the only books in the house were my textbooks. So I picked them up for the first time since the beginning of the school year. Wouldn't you know, there was a section on law in the first one I read. *American Civilization Then and Now* the book was called. I'll never forget that. I read the Declaration of Independence and parts of the Constitution. I was hooked. I didn't care that we didn't have the money for school. I thought, where there's a will, there's a way."

Goose bumps covered Grace's arms. "That's quite a story, Lone Star. You turned your life around on a dime."

"I have to tell you, I'm happy as a hog in mud I was born in West Texas. If I'd been born in your San Francisco, we'd never have lost power, and I'd probably be cleaning toilets at Whataburger."

Grace's head still sizzled like an egg in a desert frying pan, but she sweated less. Both her step and her heart felt lighter. "I don't know. I beginning to think you're the kind of guy who can do practically anything."

"My mom's the one you should admire. Pop too. He's one of the best ranch hands I've ever known. But Mom." Lone Star whistled in appreciation. "She can do anything she sets her mind to."

"Like what?"

"Like kill a rattlesnake at twenty paces."

"You're kidding me. That's way too Wild West."

"I'm not kidding. Being handy with a gun's a necessity where I grew up."

"Being handy with a gun lands you in prison where I grew up."

"How about sewing on a finger?"

"Your mom did that?"

"Sewed on Uncle Coke's finger when his hand got caught in the razor wire fence." Lone Star held up his hand. "Can't show you which one without being rude though."

"Did it work?"

"Long enough to get him to the nearest hospital, two hours away."

"Two hours? You'd drive past fifty hospitals if you drove for two hours from my house."

"Guess it's better to be sick in San Francisco, then. But I still wouldn't trade in El Paso."

"Why not?"

"My family's all there, for one. And it's the kind of country that gets under your skin. A stranger might think it's boring, but to me that landscape's as pretty as a pie supper."

Every half hour as they walked on, Lone Star called for her to stop. He handed her the water bottle, and she took a long drink.

"How about you?"

"Don't you worry none about me. In El Paso we like it hot and dry. Anyway, I have another bottle. I drink as we walk along. Saves time."

Near dusk, they reached Lake Morena County Park and descended to the campground. At the park sign, Grace's foot caught on a rock. She stumbled. Lone Star grabbed her waist and propped her up. Grace felt an unexpected jolt of adrenaline at his touch.

"Almost there. You okay to walk?"

Grace rubbed her forehead and nodded. "Sorry. I'm okay. I'm just excited to see civilization again."

"Understandable. You've been through a lot for one day. Let's get you to some shade and a long, cold shower."

Grace glanced up at the mention of the shower but saw nothing in Lone Star's face to indicate any indelicacy.

An elderly couple soon spotted the short, exhausted Asian woman shuffling alongside the tall, buff redhead with what looked like a baby carrier on his chest. They hurried over.

"We were on the lookout for hikers in need of some help." The woman took Grace's pack while the man carried Lone Star's. "You never know what the desert will cough up this time of year. You two look like you're in serious need of the joys of electricity. Ice and AC. I don't understand why anyone comes to the desert without it."

She invited them to a sizable RV. "We come here during the PCT thru-hiking season to help out. We used to be big hikers ourselves. But one thing and another. You know how it goes."

Inside, a long-haired Chihuahua pranced at the woman's feet, yipping and begging to be picked up. She scooped him into her arms and patted his head.

"Fritzy here is an indoor kind of guy. He has no idea what his mom and pop used to get up to."

She turned the air conditioning to high, filled a floral print pitcher with ice and water, and placed two large plastic cups in front of Grace and Lone Star. Lone Star drained cup after cup without speaking. Grace watched.

I could have died out there if he hadn't found me. I was so unprepared. So stupid. What am I going to do if he doesn't stick with me tomorrow?

She refilled her cup from the pitcher as Lone Star finished his sixth glass.

"Sorry, ma'am. " He wiped his mouth with his bandana. "I was feeling a bit parched."

The couple lived outside Palm Springs. Lone Star chatted with them about desert life, his family's El Paso farm, and what he'd seen on the trail. Grace relaxed in the coolness. Her mind drifted.

Kenji would never have ended up in this mess. He would have packed more water. He would have studied the risks. I'm a threat to myself, for goodness sake.

Lone Star was absorbed in a story of a rattlesnake, a pistol, and a bottle of Pepto Bismol. His freckled arms circled and waved as he drew his audience in. Grace leaned back and studied him.

Such masculine hands. Not an ounce of fat. Just muscle. A bear would think twice before attacking that body.

Lone Star paused and rocked in his chair.

"Well?" The woman leaned forward. "Don't leave us hanging."

Maybe hiking's not the kind of thing an unfit person like me should do alone. Maybe you need a partner. I could have done this before breaking up with Ben. But that would never have worked. Ben was way too competitive. He'd have said, "I'll see how much farther I can get than you today," and that would have been the last I saw of him until Canada. No Ben is good. But no one in my life isn't.

"Pink crud dripped all over him."

Grace reached for her water glass as Lone Star gestured for effect. Her arm collided with his. Water spilled across the vinyl tablecloth and her shirt.

"Aw, Just Grace, I'm so sorry." Lone Star handed her a napkin. "I should watch where these big hands of mine are flying."

Grace flushed and rubbed the blotch. "Don't worry about it. You've got great hands. I need a shower anyway. I probably smell like the elephant exhibit at the zoo."

Lone Star laughed. "Darlin', you smell as sweet as a daisy. Wait until you've been out on the trail for two weeks without so much as a rinse. Even the mosquitos won't come near you."

"I hope you still would."

"You betcha. Nothing would keep me from your side."

Lone Star gave her hand a squeeze. A warm tingle surged up her arm.

Maybe it's not just me who's thinking about us.

Outside, the evening breeze felt fresh and new.

Grace beamed at the emerging stars.

Maybe he'll stick with me after all.

Their gear lay under the motor home's blue and grey awning. She picked up one of Lone Star's shoes and peeked inside.

"Size fourteen. Wow."

She glanced at his pack. Its compression straps held her empty three-liter water bottle. On a hunch, she squatted, slid open the pack's draw cords, and felt around inside, recognizing items by touch: sleeping bag...tent stakes...headlamp...cook pot...hard candy in a plastic baggie...socks...toilet paper and trowel...harmonica?

In the depths, her hands encountered another plastic container, squashed to take up less space. She pulled it out. A second three-liter bottle. Empty.

Her heart beat quickly as her eyes registered shock.

The other bottle he said he was drinking from was empty the whole time. He never had any water out there. Just let me use up his entire supply.

She sat cross-legged on the dirt by the camper and stared at the bottle.

So, basically, when I'm on the trail, I'm not only a threat to myself, I'm a threat to others.

She rose and walked to the showers, shaking her head.

Later, after sharing a hearty dinner with the RV couple, Lone Star and Grace pitched their tents in adjacent campsites. For Grace, tent poles went into wrong grommets, stakes came loose, and clips misaligned. Lone Star set his up in a flash and sat in the entrance, watching her struggle.

"I wouldn't mind a little help here, if you've got the time."

"I've got the time. But you have to learn this for yourself, darlin'. Soon it'll be as easy as pie. But not if I do it for you. Besides, I enjoy watching you. You clean up real nice."

"Thanks." Grace curtsied. Her foot caught in a tent line and she fell. Lone Star chuckled so long he had to hold his sides.

"From where I'm sitting, Lone Star, you're not living up to Southern gentleman standards." She brushed herself off. "What's the Texas expression for go jump in a lake?"

"What I think you're trying to say is that you think I'm about as fine as cream gravy."

Grace used a rock to pound in her final tent stake and attached its guy-line. "Yes, that's what I meant." She tossed a pine cone at his head. "You're as fine as clean gravy. So is my tent. Not bad for a first try."

"Not clean gravy. Cream gravy. And it's a fine tent indeed."

Once inside her shelter, Grace was too tired to crawl into her sleeping bag. She pulled it over her like a blanket, thought for a second of Lone Star's blue eyes, and fell asleep before the cover reached her chin.

Cheerful whistling roused her when dawn was still a light orange glow on the horizon. She pushed the tent flap aside and made out Lone Star breaking camp.

"Didn't mean to wake you, darlin'."

"You're leaving? Already?" Sudden anxiety

prickled in her.

"Sure am. Today's supposed to be cooler, they say. Still, it's good to start early in the desert, no matter what the prediction."

"Wait." Grace scrambled out. "I can pack up and go with you. Quick as a caterpillar in heat. Or whatever you'd say." She wrapped her arms around herself to keep warm in the crisp morning air.

Lone Star's face shone with affection. "Just Grace, your coming with me is a sweet thought." He took gentle hold of her shoulders and turned her around. "But you crawl right back in your bag. You're staying put today."

Her attention focused on his hands as he gently pushed her toward her tent. Warm, firm, comforting hands. A sudden longing enveloped her. She struggled out of his grip. "I don't need any more rest. I'm fine."

"You don't know how tired you are."

"I'm okay. Really." She jumped up and down. "See?"

"No arguing." He again ushered her to the tent and waited until she was tightly wrapped and zipped inside. His thighs appeared at the entrance as he folded his long body until his head was level with his knees.

"I loved hiking with you yesterday, Just Grace. My heart is saying stay here with you. But I've got 2,600 miles to hike before snow lands in Canada. And my law practice isn't going to be there forever if I don't get back to it as soon as I can. I've just got to skedaddle."

He cares more about his work than he does

about me.

She fought back tears and willed her voice not to crack. "Okay. I understand. You've got your…priorities."

Lone Star reached for her chin but she jerked it away.

He let his hand drop. "Don't be that way, Just Grace. You've got to have a little faith."

"Faith in what?"

"Faith in us." He rubbed his hand against her cheek. This time she leaned into it.

"There's an us?"

"There's an us now. I'm fixin' to make sure there's an us for a good long time."

Grace's heart exploded with a warmth that shot through her. She unzipped the bag and flipped over, propping herself up on her elbows.

Lone Star stroked her hair. "You take a day or two of rest. Get going again when you feel strong and secure. Take lots of water, you hear? I think you learned your lesson yesterday, but be careful." He jerked his thumb behind him. "It's so dry out there, even the catfish are carrying canteens."

Grace raised her eyebrows, feeling suddenly playful. "I think I saw some of those yesterday."

"They're out there if you look for them."

"Are you done with the advice?"

"No. When you meet more experienced hikers, listen to what they tell you. You're still green."

She wriggled partly out of her bag. "Why don't you just slow your pace a little? I'll hike faster, I promise."

"Whoa, there." Lone Star held up his hand. "I

thought we had that settled. On the trail, your legs and mine aren't constructed to go the same speed. Listen, Just Grace. There's something on the trail called magic. Like when a man with water finds a woman with none. But the thing about trail magic is that you can't hold on to it forever. On the trail, you sometimes have to let go."

A tear escaped the corner of Grace's eye.

Lone Star swept it away with his finger. He rubbed his nose, blinked, and pulled the blue bandana from around his neck, using it to wipe his eyes. "Darn dust."

He held out his hand. Her tiny fingers disappeared in his. His long, unblinking look telegraphed strength, comfort, and something else.

Passion?

"Look for my name in the hiker registers in the towns up the trail. I'll leave you a note in every one. And, who knows? Maybe down the road a bit, I'll take a couple of days off, and you'll catch up with me."

"You promise?"

"I promise. Nothing will keep me from seeing you again."

He squeezed her hand and rose.

A tiny drum beat a strong, persistent rhythm against the wall of her chest. From her sleeping bag, she watched his hiking shoes disappear from view. Only exhaustion prevented her from jumping up and clutching him to her.

CHAPTER 5

Lone Star's stride intermittently quickened then slackened for the first hours after leaving Grace that morning. At points he turned around and retraced his steps for a few yards before turning again and surging forward.

What am I doing leaving her back there alone? She needs me. Heck, I need her.

He swung south toward Lake Morena.

But this ain't my first rodeo. I know how this goes. Getting back together will be all the sweeter because we've been apart for a while.

He reversed direction and headed north again.

His mind ricocheted between two warring impulses such that the scenery, normally an integral part of his awareness, could have changed to skyscrapers, icebergs, or rocket ships. He wouldn't have noticed.

Why didn't I meet her back in Texas? Sure, I'm always at work. Could have met her at a trial, though. Grace Mori, public school psychologist, sued for encouraging kids to bother their parents with questions instead of keeping quiet in front of a video game.

Something bumped his arm, jerking his mind back to the desert.

"Excuse me." A teenage girl with a blonde pixie cut held up her hand in apology. "I tried to get out of your way, but you stepped right into me."

Lone Star wiped his hand in front of his face, as if trying to clean away cobwebs. "Completely my fault, little missy. My mind was busy as a one-armed paper hanger. Just didn't see you."

He turned to face a group of four girls, all wearing maroon '*Julian High School Volleyball*' shirts.

Lone Star pointed. "Where's Julian?"

One girl turned to show him her backpack, embroidered with multiple renditions of pie crusts and fillings. "You've never heard of Julian apple pie? You can't be from California."

"Do I sound like I'm from California, darlin'?" Lone Star chuckled. "What's the famous Julian apple pie volleyball team doing out here in the Mojave? Playing catch with armadillos?"

The girls nudged each other. The one who'd spoken first stepped forward a little. "I'm Amber. This is Emily, Brianna, and Taylor. Emily's captain of the varsity team. It was her idea to come out here."

Emily shook her head quickly. "*Was* captain."

"So it's a graduation trip for you gals?"

"Sort of." Emily glanced at her teammates. "My girl scout troop did a day-hike on the PCT a few years ago. It was awesome. I always wanted to come back, but my parents never thought it was a good idea."

"She talked it up *a lot*." Amber widened her eyes and spread her hands far apart.

Lone Star nodded. "Does it live up to expectations?"

All four girls chimed in at once. Lone Star made out "awesome," "sweet," "seriously scary," and "best three days of my life."

Amber looked up at him. "Why are *you* out here?"

"I'm a thru."

Open mouths greeted his announcement. Lone Star suppressed a chuckle with a well-timed cough.

"A thru." The complete silence of her friends accentuated Amber's whisper. "Awesome. We were saying this whole time we wanted to meet one."

"Now don't go making my head swell. I haven't reached Canada yet."

"But you're going to try." The amazement in Brianna's voice brought a light blush to Lone Star's cheeks.

"Talk to me in a few months, *bonita chica*."

In unison, the girls flung off their backpacks and scrabbled inside. One by one they held up their cell phones.

"You want my…" Lone Star paused.

"Facebook page."

"Instagram username."

"Twitter handle."

"Pinterest account."

As the words tumbled out of their mouths, Lone Star wrinkled his mouth and squinted with one eye.

"I hate disappointing you all. Work email's the best I can do. And I won't be checking that for months."

The girls' faces fell.

"That's okay." Amber punched her phone a few times and handed it to him. "Put your contact information in here."

Lone Star took the phone with both hands and typed slowly, hitting the delete key almost as often as he hit the letters.

Amber glanced at what he'd written before her fingers flew over the display. "Mr. Hogan, from El Paso. I'll put a note in my calendar to email you in August, okay?"

"That'll inspire me."

Amber glanced again at her phone. "Our parents are going to meet us at Lake Morena in a few hours. We've got to get going, Mr. Hogan. It was awesome meeting you." She held out her hand and shook Lone Star's with enthusiasm.

"Wait. Group photo."

After Brianna squeezed them all together for a selfie, the girls jogged down the trail, turning back periodically to wave at Lone Star.

When they had shrunk to images the size of his hand, he turned back to the trail and marched forward with firm steps. "Well, now, wasn't that all sweetness and light? Nothing like a little youthful enthusiasm to put the spring back in my step."

That evening, an unfamiliar sound brought him out of his tent a final time into the chilly semi-darkness of a full moon. He shone his headlamp around the perimeter of his campsite, looking and listening.

Someone's running.

An outline of a short, thin figure approached. Lone Star cupped his hands. "Grace? Just Grace, darlin', is that you? Don't run. I'm here."

A gravelly falsetto answered back. "Not Grace, sweetie."

Lone Star switched off his headlamp to let his eyes adjust. The man halted next to him, breathing deeply.

"Sorry to disappoint. Seems like you were expecting someone else."

Lone Star held the back of his neck with his hand. "Now that's embarrassing."

The runner's teeth flashed white in the dark as his face split into a grin. "Not at all. First time I've been mistaken for a woman. I'll take it as a compliment."

"Not everyone would." Lone Star clasped his hands in front of him. "Name's Lone Star. Where you headed?"

"Shadow. Going to Canada."

Lone Star whistled. "Whoo-wee. Look what the cat dragged in. Read about you on the listserv. Go so fast that all people see is your shadow. I count myself real lucky."

Shadow put his hands on his hips and marched in place. "Somebody gave me the name and it stuck. Not sure that's why, though."

"Modesty. Like that in a man."

"Just hiking my own hike. We've all got our reasons for being out here. I got tired of ultra marathons. The PCT seemed like a logical next step."

Lone Star shoved his hands into the pockets of his down vest. "Is this your first thru-hike?"

"No. I did it last year. This year I'm going for the record."

"Thought I remembered that." Lone Star stepped off the trail. "I don't want to hold you up."

Shadow switched to stretching, standing first on one leg, then the other. "No worries, man. I got time. Don't get to talk to a lot of people. Why are you out here?"

Lone Star cocked his head to the side and looked at the dark rim of distant mountains. "I'm thirty-five and felt kind of burned out at work. Spending most days sitting at a desk looking out my window isn't what I imagined when I picked a law career."

"Thought it would involve more work in the woods?" The moonlight highlighted Shadow's teeth, exposed in a wide smile.

"Thought I'd have more free time, I guess." Lone Star shifted his weight from foot to foot. "I always loved hiking. When I was a kid, my whole family would go on overnights. In the summers, we'd even go for a week. Those were some of the best times of my life. Being with family and being outdoors."

"What happened?"

"Nothing. My family still goes on the trips. Only the last two times they went, I couldn't. Had too much work."

Shadow groaned. "That sucks, man."

Lone Star picked up a rock and threw it into the distance. "It set my priorities straight. Told my boss she could either give me five months unpaid leave or find herself a new lead attorney."

"Did she cave?"

"Mostly. She gave me four months. So now I'm hiking against the clock. But at least I'm out here."

Shadow returned to marching in place. "Hiking against the clock's not so bad."

"Got any tips?"

"Go ultralight. My base weight's eight pounds." He looked at Lone Star's camp site. "No tent or sleeping bag. Only a tarp and quilt."

The nylon of his shelter fluttered as Lone Star kicked at a guy-line. "I've come a long way already, believe it or not. My family used to take a huge Army surplus monstrosity. Had to carry it one year. Nearly broke my back."

"Tents aren't all bad. Maybe you're planning on having company in there from time to time."

"The only one I'd want for company I left back at Lake Morena."

"Let me guess. Grace?"

"Just Grace." The bracing night air carried the scent of nearby sage brush, reminding Lone Star of where he'd met her. "Ever feel like you're making a mistake?"

"Often. But never on the trail."

The two men both looked at the dirt. Shadow began jogging in place. "Afraid I've got to get going. The night air chills me if I don't keep moving."

"How many miles till you make camp?"

"Don't know yet. The trail tells me when to stop."

Lone Star reached out his hand and shook

Shadow's. "Good lesson for us all. Been a pleasure talking with you, Shadow." The dark shape disappeared into the desert night long before the reverberating *thud, thud* of his footsteps died out. Lone Star stood and stared after him until the cold drove him back inside.

Good night, Just Grace. This trail will bring us together again. You can count on it.

CHAPTER 6

Early in May of the previous year, west of Oakland's technical high school, Jerry Kriebel rolled his new mountain bike home toward the dingy single-family house he shared with seven acquaintances. Strong California sunshine reflected off the shiny metal.

He lumbered up cracked cement stairs carrying his purchase, a plastic Stoke's Spokes bag dangling from the handlebars. He leaned the bike against the living room wall next to the TV, grabbed a beer from the kitchen, and spread out an assortment of new gear on the grungy living room carpet. Biking shorts, shirt, helmet, gloves, and a hydration pack covered the threadbare floor. An extreamly tall young man in shorts and an oversize shirt walked through the room.

"Shit, dude." Jerry's roommate examined the acquisitions with obvious envy. "You got yourself some banging stuff."

Jerry grinned. "If I can find a ride to Marin County tomorrow, I'm gonna take this baby out on the trails. See what she can do."

"Sweet." The friend stroked the bike's gleaming surface. "Bet you could do sixty down a good hill."

"Yep. Way better than my crap car."

"Your crap car's totaled."

"That's why I got the bike."

"Bike's a better fit for those stubby legs of yours anyway." The friend punched Jerry's arm. "If you need a ride to Marin, Rasta might let you borrow his pickup. If you get it back before dark."

"Got no license, dude, remember?"

"Don't think Rasta'll mind. He probably even knows where you should go. Just don't total his shagging wagon."

They snickered at the shared joke of their roommate's consistent failure to get any of his short-lived girlfriends to join him in the bed of his pickup, where he optimistically kept a mattress.

The next morning, Jerry drove the pickup out of Oakland, crossed the Bay Bridge, meandered through fog-encased San Francisco and across the Golden Gate Bridge, and entered Marin. He was grateful for the stinking mattress protecting his new bike in the back of the truck as he navigated bumps in the pavement. The truck wound up Shoreline Highway and then along Panoramic. The Pacific Ocean lay to the left. But a dense white mist hung in the trees over the embankment.

All these clouds. Can't even see the ocean. It's like I'm on top of the world.

Jerry negotiated the sharp turns and steep inclines with squealing tires, often veering across the dividing line into the opposing lane. At seven on a Sunday morning, he encountered few other drivers.

The GPS on his phone recalculated when he passed the Mountain Home Inn on Mount Tamalpais. He swerved on the fire road to the north and shot into the empty parking lot across the street. After dressing in bike gear in the front seat, he threw his street in the footwell. The cool air made him wish for a long-sleeved shirt. But it had seemed so unnecessary in sunny Oakland.

He tucked his shoulder-length hair under his helmet, then pedaled up the fire road's wide dirt expanse.

Jerry rode toward the summit of Mount Tam like an agitated crab, all at right angles. Elbows pointed to the sky, short legs jutted to the sides, torso bent forward. Bulging eyes focused on the trail ahead. Sweat beaded on his forehead as he puffed for air. After ten minutes, he stopped.

Screw all this climbing. I'm wiped.

He jerked his handlebars to the side, nearly lost his balance, recovered, and pointed the bike downhill.

"Now this is more like it." He leaned forward and shifted into high gear. His legs pedaled furiously, increasing his pace.

The bike bounced across small rocks and dirt, skidding from side to side. It slithered around a turn. Jerry dropped his foot, scraping a long, thin line in the sand. The shrubbery and trees sped past his peripheral vision in a blur. Before long, he arrived back at Panoramic Highway. He turned down the first road he saw. There, the initial descent petered out quickly and his pace slowed as the street meandered past multi-million dollar houses perched on the hillside.

Who the fuck lives here?

He passed gated driveways with surveillance cameras and mysterious steps leading to impenetrable fences. Occasionally, beat up cars hugged the side of the road.

Must be the cleaning ladies' cars. People around here drive Beemers and Ferraris.

As if to prove him right, a gleaming black metalic Mercedes SL Roadster pulled around a corner. Jerry braked. The balding man in the convertible gave him a wave as he roared past.

Jerry returned the wave with a salute.

Sweet ride.

Around another corner, he saw what he had been looking for: a narrow dirt and gravel footpath sloping steeply downhill.

Awesome.

He swerved onto the trail.

Now this is effing mountain biking.

The wheels bounced precariously and threatened to throw him off. Lattices of exposed roots and large rocks jutted out at unexpected intervals. Jerry braked, tipped, and seesawed down the path. He grazed a tree. Vines and brush that clung to the upside of the hill clutched at him as he sped past.

A little more lift and I'll take right off. Who said mountain biking is difficult? I've got natural talent. With a little practice I'll probably make a team.

A large rock jerked his thoughts back to the trail. His front tire spun. He caught a brief glimpse of the steep ravine to his left.

Don't want to end up down there.

His feet pushed the bike to quicken its pace. He rounded a sharp corner.

The next instant, the world moved in slow motion. Flash of blue. Handlebars yanked right. Fingers clenched. Eyes closed. Tires skidding. Body off seat. Bike into hillside. Head back. Shoulder into protruding root. Pain down arm. Leg pinned to slope.

Ouch.

Jerry moved his arm.

That hurts.

He wiggled his fingers.

Don't think anything's broken.

Then his leg.

I'm okay.

He stood.

Christ, that was lucky. I could have gone over the handlebars. And down the cliff.

He reoriented himself.

Then he heard screaming.

"Kaylee!" A woman's voice rose from the woods below him, drifting up through the grey mist. "Kaylee! Are you all right? Kaylee, answer me!"

Jerry pushed his bike back onto the trail and returned to the spot where he'd been knocked off balance. He peered over the edge of the cliff and glimpsed a curled hand. A crumpled body. Sky blue shorts from which protruding legs twisted obscenely, like a mutilated doll. The back of a torn white jacket patched with a crimson that deepened as he watched.

"Kaylee!" The shouting neared.

Jerry grabbed his bike.

The girl's beyond help. Save my own ass. That's always the best plan.

He ran up the hill, shoving his bike ahead of him.

"Stop! You hit Kaylee."

The cries urged him on. Jerry clambered erratically up the trail. His feet toppled over roots. The bike wheels snagged on bushes. He plowed ahead, fueled by fear and adrenaline. The shrieks grew fainter.

When he reached the pavement, Jerry jumped on the seat. The road flashed under his tires as he put distance between himself and the broken girl. Back at the highway, a few cars filled the parking spaces beside his truck. He slid to a stop beside it, hefted his bike, and tossed it onto the lumpy mattress without an ounce of his prior pride or care.

"Easy, dude, easy." He gunned the engine. His heart pounded in his head like thunder. His hands sweated through the bike gloves. He floored the accelerator.

His breathing didn't return to normal until he stopped for gas at a Sunoco on a crowded US 101 near San Jose, seventy miles south of Mount Tam. The pimply clerk in the stained Pro-Pain punk band t-shirt admired Jerry's biking gear when he paid for an extra large Dr. Pepper and three Snickers bars.

"Forget you ever saw me." Jerry handed the guy a twenty.

"Sure, dude. Never saw you." The boy pocketed the bill and looked away.

Have to get out of these clothes. Nobody looks at

a regular guy in a pickup.

Jerry got his street clothes and changed in the dingy men's room where toilet paper littered the floor and lewd graffiti mocked him from the walls. Then he called his housemate from the front seat of the truck.

"Tell Rasta I'm driving his pickup to LA. Tell him to chill out about the money. I'll wire him some by the end of the week. And don't spread this around, okay? I had this urge to go south for a while. I'll call again when I get there." He hung up quickly and dialed his cousin in Milwaukee.

"Don't you have a friend in an LA band?" A car pulled into the parking lot and Jerry slouched lower in his seat.

"Yeah. My girlfriend's roommate's got a brother in a band. Mega Oil Spill. Why?"

"Can you give me his number? I'm heading to LA and I need a place to crash."

"No problem." His cousin put down the phone and Jerry listened to the muffled conversation of two voices. When he returned to the receiver, he gave Jerry the number. "Hey, dude, I don't want to ask questions, but you in some kind of trouble? Last I heard from you, you were liking Oakland."

"Just need a change. But if anyone asks, you haven't heard from me."

"Sure." His cousin paused. "Something you want me to tell your folks if they ask?"

"They been asking?"

"Nope."

"They ever asked?"

"Nope."

"So you got your answer. Bet they don't even realize I left Milwaukee."

"It's all good, dude. You got some ranking times coming your way in LA. I can feel it."

The seven-hour drive to LA gave Jerry time to think.

First, don't speed. Last thing I need is a cop who looks at my license and punches me into a police computer. Second, when I get to LA, I'll need cash. So I'll sell the bike. Even if I only get half what it's worth. The sooner I get rid of it, the better. Probably has something disgusting from that girl on it. I'll sell this truck while I'm at it. That'll give me enough to send to Rasta. With probably some left over.

Interstate 5 traffic inched into the city bumper to bumper. His dented truck jostled for position with lipstick red Ferraris and utilitarian grey Prius hatchbacks. Drivers shared middle finger gestures as they cut each other off. Jerry relaxed.

There's no way the trouble I left on the mountain will follow me here. To the land of movie stars. The land of money. One day soon, I'll be driving one of those Ferraris.

For now, I'll get stoned. Get that crumpled girl out of my mind. Back in Milwaukee, I was always good at forgetting things.

***

The following afternoon, Ed Galeano looked up from behind Stoke's Spokes bike shop counter as the door chime rang. Streaming sunlight framed the dark silhouette of a uniformed police officer.

"Good afternoon. My name's Turangeo. From the Mill Valley Police Department. I'm looking for Edmundo Galeano, the owner."

Ed's eyes narrowed slightly, visions of previous encounters with the police briefly flooding his thoughts. He took a breath. "That's me. What can I do for you?"

"There was a mountain bike accident yesterday on Mount Tamalpais." The officer paused, advanced a stride, and appraised Ed's face.

Must have been one of my customers, Ed thought.

He relaxed and stepped from behind the desk. "How can I help?"

The officer hung his thumbs from his belt. "A nine-year-old girl was run off a trail on Mount Tam. She's in critical condition." Again, he paused and scanned Ed. "Her mother saw someone on a mountain bike. We think it was the person who ran her down."

Ed nodded.

"Someone identified you at the scene of the crime, Mr. Galeano. So I have a few questions. Is there a room where we can talk?"

CHAPTER 7

I never got his real name.

The thought jerked Grace awake. She shook off the sleeping bag and pitched out of her tent, thinking hard about where she was and where Lone Star had gone.

Lake Morena County Park. Lone Star left. Without me.

She hurriedly packed her tent and filled water canisters at a bathroom sink. Her hands still dripped and gear threatened to fall out of her half-closed pack as she raced past rows of campers where scents of bacon and cinnamon drifted on the early morning air.

Wait, Lone Star.

But before she reached the park entrance, her thigh muscles cramped. Her fingers numbed. Surrounding trees greyed and swayed.

Oh, no.

Shaky knees gave way, and her back slid down a pine tree trunk to the dusty ground.

***

"What am I going to do without him?" Grace watched her new friend back at the RV cook breakfast, inhaling the sweet odor of pancakes that pervaded the trailer. "I almost killed myself out there. Now I'm terrified I'm going to do it again. Although it won't be for lack of water. I'm filling all my containers I have to the brim. I don't care if I look like an elephant."

"Sweetie, I always told my kids, if you fall off a bicycle, you have to get right back on. Or else you'll be scared of bikes for the rest of your life."

She presented Grace with a stack of pancakes. Grace sniffed the steam, reminded of home.

"I don't know if that applies in this situation." Grace positioned knife and fork to slice into the heap. "I mean, the trail's not like a bike. More like a living thing. Like if you get bitten by a dog. You don't run back and try to pet it again, do you? Maybe the trail bit me. So maybe I shouldn't keep going. Maybe I should hitch a ride to the next resupply stop and get my bearings before I continue."

The older woman put her hands on her hips. "Or get to the next resupply stop and catch Lone Star?"

"I don't usually act like a stalker. But I don't even know his real name. What if something happens and I can't find him again?"

"Look, dear, if that's what you want to do, you should do it." She shrugged and turned back to the stove. "Go find Lone Star. But I thought he promised to keep in touch."

"He did."

"Well, you and he can't hike together anyway. So what's the point of rushing up the trail to see him again for an hour, when he's going to leave you behind again? If you ask me…" She stopped and occupied herself with peeling an orange. "I'm sorry. I'm handing out unasked for advice. You didn't ask me, did you? Ralph always says I put my nose in where it doesn't belong." She handed Grace fruit sections on a paper plate.

"Go right ahead." Grace put down her utensils and waited.

"Well, you were talking about a dog. I think if a dog bites you, maybe you had bad luck. Maybe you aren't experienced with dogs. So get out there and meet a few more. Play with them. Before you know it, you'll have a dog as your best friend." She refilled Grace's coffee cup. "If you let someone else do all the interacting, you'll never get the hang of it yourself."

So the trail's a dog? Grace thought later as she sat in the park ranger station, poring over the contents of the hiker box. *And I should go out and make nice with it?*

The black plastic bin in front of her contained an assortment of hikers' discarded clothing, food, and equipment. The sign above it indicated anyone was free to sift through what others had left. She held up a partnerless dirty sock.

Yech.

She rummaged more.

Strange thing is, as bad as yesterday was, it was also amazing.

56

She sorted through thick winter gloves, insect repellant, and heavy items of every description. A bottle of hand lotion. A Bowie knife. A small battery-operated radio. A couple of mystery novels. She even found two dozen chocolate chip power bars melted into outlandish shapes.

Grace's own contributions included batteries, deodorant, rice cakes, and the two-pound bear-proof canister the park ranger insisted she wouldn't need until the Sierra Mountains. She also abandoned over half her food.

My first resupply box is waiting at the Mount Laguna store, only a day long day of hiking up the trail.

When she lifted her pack to leave the station, a chuckle escaped her lips. She turned to the ranger standing behind the counter. "This weighs a lot less."

The uniformed man nodded encouragingly. "You're gonna be happy you did that. Take care of the ounces, and the pounds will take care of themselves."

Grace gave him a wry smile. "I learned my lesson yesterday. From now on, I'm making as much room as possible for water."

"Wait." The ranger raised a hand. "You're the woman who came in with heat exhaustion?"

"Word travels fast. I'm afraid I am."

"Then I've got something for you. Hold on." The man disappeared into a back room and emerged a minute later holding a green plastic water bottle stamped '*San Diego County Parks and Recreation.*' "It's not new, but I washed it out." He wiped the outside with a paper towel. "It's to remind you how lucky you were." He handed it to Grace. Grace hesitated. "Go ahead. I can get another back at the main office any day."

"Thanks. It'll be my good luck charm."

"Everybody needs a little extra help now and then. In less than two weeks, the park's hosting the annual kick off party for the PCT hiking season. After that, there'll be more people on the trail. You won't be so isolated." He scratched his chin. "I worry about you novices, coming from all over the world to hike in one of the most inhospitable places this country has to offer. I had a guy from Finland early last summer. He'd never been in temperatures above eighty before. He didn't take enough water either. Had to be medivaced out. Almost didn't make it." His eyebrows drew together. "You take care, okay?"

"I promise I won't make any headlines."

Grace stood outside the ranger station, looking at the water bottle.

Here in the park, it's easy to forget I'm in a desert. Cabins, bathrooms, and showers. A playground and a boat launch. Motor homes with water and electricity hookups. But I know what it's really like out there.

She added an extra gallon of water to her pack before she set out the following morning. The elderly couple and their Chihuahua walked her to the end of the road. The woman wrote her phone number on a scrap of paper that she slipped to Grace.

"We live in Palm Springs, dear. Got a small

house with a guest room and a pool. You're always welcome. And if you get into any kind of trouble, call us, day or night. We're usually up past midnight playing cards anyway."

Grace's stride leaving the park was almost as light as it had been at the Mexican border.

I thought this hike was going to be boring. Instead, I spend years looking for that special someone in bars and online, and we find each other under a tree in the middle of nowhere.Now all I have to do is not fall too far behind.

At nine in the morning, she stopped at the Boulder Oaks Campground for a snack in the shade. She removed her shoes and socks and tiptoed to the bathroom to rinse her burning feet, lifting one at a time into the sink.

Okay, Lone Star. Now I see what you were doing. Distracting me from the pounding my feet are taking. Rolling hills and never-ending chaparral seemed a lot more interesting when I was talking with you.

She replaced her footwear and returned to the trail.

Did Kenji know what hiking in the desert's like? She trudged through the dust. *Pitiless sun, scorching heat, and interminable monotony? And, to be fair, vistas in twenty shades of brown. Green, six-inch lizards basking on rocks. Cacti shadows that flicker at dusk. Okay, it's not so bad.*

She tripped in a mouse hole and stumbled into bushes, scraping her arms and legs.

Or maybe it is. What did he think he was going to get out of this? And what the heck goes through

Lone Star's mind as he's walking out here?

She saw a large footprint in the path. Her heart fluttered.

Is he slowing down so I can catch up to him?

She sped up. After hours of hard, persistent, and solitary climbing, Grace spent the night at a campground a few miles short of her first resupply stop.

My soles feel like I've been walking on hot coals. I'm sure Lone Star's long gone already. And that Mount Laguna store is probably closed. Don't want to make a wasted trip.

After pitching her tent and cooking her first trail dinner, she shone her headlamp on her feet. Several enormous, festering blisters stared accusingly at her.

Wow. I've gotten blisters with a new pair of pumps, but these are larger than a Texas hippo's backside, or whatever Lone Star would say. I'll wear my camp shoes tonight. Maybe they'll disappear.

They didn't.

Grace hobbled onto the porch of the Mount Laguna store before eight the next morning. Four bearded, smelly hikers greeted her with high fives. The contents of their backpacks plastered the ragged wooden floorboards. The twenty-somethings pawed through the contents of the hiker box.

"We're looking for anything we can yogi."

Yogi?

"How did I miss you guys on the trail yesterday?" Grace pushed aside a pack to sit on the edge of the porch.

"We hiked straight through from Lake Morena.

Must have leapfrogged your tent." A freckled teenager winked at her. "We got here right at closing and stayed in that cabin over there. Too bad you weren't here to join us for the vodka shots." He patted an empty bottle next to him.

I remember their type from college. Fun-loving, but not reliable. Still, I could use some advice.

Keen faces crowded around her dangling feet. Fingers examined and prodded the blisters. Different people offered solutions.

The consensus was that while blisters were serious business out on the trail, Grace was in luck. Hers hadn't broken open and bled. But judgments divided about the best treatment. To pop or not to pop. To build a small wall of foam around each one, or to cover the entire surface with foam. To hold bandages in place using duct tape or surgical tape. Grace held her head in her hands.

"Who knew blister care was as controversial as fracking?"

A gravelly voice interrupted the heated debate. "Hope you don't mind my butting in. But I think you need to give your feet a rest. I suggest you get a cabin for tonight, one with a bathtub. Soak your feet. Then take another look in the morning. Don't use duct tape if you can avoid it. Thrus love it, but the adhesive is nasty stuff."

The voice had a distinctly Midwestern ring to it. Grace looked behind her, expecting to see a grizzled farmer in overalls with a corncob pipe jutting from his mouth. An athletic, handsome man of about sixty in tan hiking pants and a lightweight, long-sleeved shirt returned her glance. Blue gaiters with white stars protected his shoes. He smiled benevolently and swung a day pack across his back.

"Good luck." He jerked his chin, saluting Grace. "Next time, stop as soon as you feel any kind of pain. Treat anything that could become a blister like it is a blister, and you'll be in better shape." To the guys congregated on the porch he waved a hand. "See you soon. I'm sure you'll leapfrog me in no time."

"Who was that?" Grace stared after him.

The young men answered in unison. "Eagle."

"Used to be a banker. Now he's a trail angel." The freckled youth smiled at her.

"Do you have to talk in code? I can't understand half of what you're saying."

"A trail angel is someone who helps thrus." The young man edged closer as his companions returned to examining the hiker box. "You know, thru-hikers. Like you. Someone hiking *through* from Mexico to Canada. Trail angels pick them up at the airport and take them out to the trailhead and stuff. Some let you sleep at their house."

"I met a couple like that at Lake Morena. This guy does it too? He volunteers? Or is it some kind of National Park Service job?"

"He does it for free, of course. If he didn't do it out of the goodness of his heart, he wouldn't be an angel." The youth tapped his heart, then let his hand fall lightly on Grace's shoulder, as if by accident.

"Right." Grace ignored his touch and looked around the porch. "So are all of you...thrus?"

"Naw, we're section hikers. Doing a piece of the trail on a long weekend. We're in school. We do this during breaks." He's grin widened as he hesitatingly stroked Grace's back. "It's too bad you weren't here with us last night."

This guy has no idea I'm almost old enough to be his mother.

Grace hopped off the porch. "Be careful what you wish for." She entered the store.

Later, in her one-room cabin, she soaked her feet in the bathtub.

How am I going to get to Canada at the rate I'm going? One day on and one day off? I can't make this a habit.

She thought back to Lone Star's message in the hiker register at the store.

Thinking of you a lot, Just Grace, and wishing our legs were walking this path side by side. You stay careful, bonita chica! I'll write you a longer note next time. Tonight I'm too tuckered out. Sweet dreams.

Grace wiped sudden beads of perspiration from her upper lip. She dunked her head under the water and came up laughing.

The next morning, her blisters felt better. But her pack felt heavier. She scrolled through the maps on her phone.

Next resupply stop's almost seventy miles north. No more water running freely from a tap. Only a few water caches and streams. Also a few horse trough options. Hope I won't have to use those.

The PCT looped around and across bare, dome-shaped hills. Occasionally, hikers passed her. When she tried to keep up with them, she fell quickly behind.

My legs aren't only too short for Lone Star. They're simply too short.

Choir Master, a fiftyish section hiker, caught up to Grace early one morning on a long, barren stretch. The man's round face, bulging stomach, and thick legs made an incongruous contrast to the skinny thrus Grace had gotten used to seeing. He paused a moment to catch his breath.

"I'm on my way to completing the entire PCT in five years' worth of long weekends." His chest expanded and contracted at a concerning pace. "Saw your signature in the Laguna Store's register. Wondered if I could catch up with you. I hate hiking alone. It's so much more fun to have somebody to talk to." Soft circles of flesh nearly obscured his eyes when he smiled. He reached out a spongy hand.

Scents of summer grass and Choir Master's sunblock mixed in the dry air. Grace took in the baggy shorts and sweat-stained shirt.

He looks like someone who could use a friend. I wouldn't mind some company for a change. It's weird not having anyone to text or talk to.

"Do you like singing? I always find it's fun to sing." He strode alongside her. Grace didn't have time to respond before he launched into a high-pitched rendition of "The Happy Wanderer." The warbling sounded familiar, but she didn't recognize the lyrics.

He's singing in German.

"Do you know it?" He stroked his triple chins as someone else might stroke a beard. "It's such a wonderful hiking song. It works well as a round. I'll teach it to you so we can sing together. Sometimes I sing it all afternoon. Right through supper time."

Oh, no.

She shook her head. "I usually like listening to sounds of the trail. Birds and animals. It's always so peaceful and quiet."

"I understand. Nothing like the sounds of nature to make you feel like singing. So how about 'The Other Day I Met a Bear?' That's a real classic. Everyone knows that one. The other day…" He paused. "Come on now. You must know it." He swung his fleshy arms from side to side in rhythm with the tune. "I sing, 'The other day,' and you repeat, 'The other day.' Then I sing, 'I met a bear,' and then you sing, 'I met a bear.' It's easy."

Grace shrugged her shoulders and joined in, mumbling the words in a hushed soprano.

So glad no one's here to post this on Facebook.

She trudged behind Choir Master in a wake of dust. The next song was "Doe a Deer" from *The Sound of Music*. Then loud performances of "This Land is Your Land" and "Cottage in a Wood," the latter complete with intricate hand gestures. By the time Choir Master reached the fifth verse of "Rise and Shine" she was rehearsing tactful ways to tell him she would rather hike alone.

She stopped for a bathroom break, urging him to go ahead without her. But he waited. She retied her shoes. He waited. She filtered water from a hopelessly shallow stream. He serenaded her with "Singing in the Rain" while her filter float bobbed in half an inch of water. She feigned a limp, and he offered his chubby shoulder as a support. No matter how slowly she hiked, saying she was holding him back, he stuck to her like a burr.

"I'm beat." She dropped her pack on a flat area near the trail at three in the afternoon. "I know you have to go on. You told me you have to finish this section by Monday."

Choir Master's face reddened with the sting of rejection. Grace avoided looking at him. She pulled her tent out of her pack and expertly flipped the poles. The inner elastic cord sprung them together with a snap.

He took a few steps, then turned around. "I'll hike slowly and keep singing, so you know where to find me if you change your mind."

I made the right decision.

She lay for a long time on her mat, looking up through mosquito netting at the endless blue of the sky. The hushed sounds of the desert exhilarated her. Beetles skittered across pebbles. Unidentified birds settled on rocky outcroppings. Bees hummed, investigating her gear. She imagined Lone Star lying next to her. Then drifted off. When she awoke, she thought she saw an extra large pair of boots outside her tent flap.

Shoot. They're only rocks.

Over the following week, the regular routine of walking, eating, and sleeping condensed her days to the essentials. The vast and severe landscape offered up intimate surprises, like a yellow flower thrusting its head between two rocks like a miniature sun, dew sparkling on her tent tie downs, and luminescent spider webs at dawn. A constant monologue heavily peppered with "Lone Star" kept her company.

Grace left the trail fifteen miles from Idyllwild, her next resupply stop, and stuck out her thumb when she reached the road.

I've never hitchhiked. But Lone Star's note is waiting for me in the hiker register. Nothing short of Norman Bates is going to keep me from getting there.

A white Chevy Camaro pulled to the side of the road almost immediately. Grace coughed and fanned at the dirt as she ran to the passenger side. A handsome square face beneath close-cropped hair leaned toward her through the window.

"Where are you heading?"

"Idyllwild."

"Then hop in the back, honey." His face disappeared behind quickly rising grey tinted glass.

Grace opened the rear passenger door a crack. "In the spirit of full disclosure, I haven't showered for a week. I don't want to get your car smelly. I'll understand if you don't want to give me a ride."

"Sweetie, you obviously haven't thumbed before." The driver, a lanky, greying man so tall that his head bowed slightly under the low roof, waved her toward the back seat. "You get in first and let the driver get going. *Then* you tell him anything that might make him change his mind. So don't let all our AC mix with your hot desert air. Get in."

Grace yanked off her pack and threw it in the back seat before hopping in behind it.

The passenger stuck out his hand. "I'm Marlowe and this is Alphonse. We're heading back to LA after a week in Palm Springs."

Grace took in the manicured fingernails as she shook the firm warm hand with her grimy own. "I'm worried I'm going to stain this seat with my sweaty shorts."

Marlowe giggled. "Never mind. It's a rental. And you're so much more interesting than the audio book we were listening to. Alphonse, we got ourselves a real live hiker."

Marlowe twisted farther in his seat to get a better look at her. "Why don't you drive if you want to go to Canada? Or how about the train?"

Their questions only stopped when she got out at the grocery store. Twenty minutes later, when she emerged swinging Fairway Foods shopping bags stuffed with snacks and half gallons of chocolate ice cream, she found the two men still seated on the hood of their car.

"We changed our plans, honey." Alphonse opened the trunk. "We called a local B&B. We're spending the night here so we can escort you back to the trail tomorrow morning. You're too cute to be trying to get rides at the side of the road. You never know what might happen."

Grace hoisted her bags in next to the leather luggage. "I'm unlikely to appeal given my stinking condition."

"You obviously don't get around too much." Marlowe nudged Alphonse in the ribs. "There's a whole seedy underworld in this country. Man or woman. Stinky or dirty. You might be just what they're looking for."

"If you're right, then that's an underworld I can do without." Grace sniffed hesitantly in the direction of her armpit. "Phew. Anyone who likes the way I smell right now needs their head examined."

"So where to next? Shower?"

"If you don't mind, I want to stop by the post office first. They've got a hiker register. I'm kind of eager to see if there's a message for me."

"Ah, a woman of mystery. We love it." The three climbed into the Camaro. "Post office it is."

The next day, Grace watched the white car disappear over the horizon at the Pines-to-Palms Highway trailhead. Bright sunshine warmed her arms as she waved. As the smell of exhaust faded, she inhaled deeply.

Then she turned on her phone and took a hundredth look at the photo of Lone Star's note.

Darling Just Grace,

I turn around whenever someone comes up behind me, hoping it's you. Do you forgive me for leaving you behind? This is just a temporary separation, I promise. Something we'll look back on fondly someday. Because you've already dug your way deep into my heart. I think of you ever so much. I've even begun composing a poem for you:

The leaves that rustle in the breeze
Remind me of your hair.
Your lips were parched, your skin so fair,
Your stride had lost its ease.

That's as far as I've gotten. I'll continue in the next note.

Picture me giving you a long hug. And more.

Missing you,
Lone Star

I've dug into his heart.

The idea tickled a mysterious spot in Grace's belly and a quick laugh burst from her, as it had every time she'd read the note.

The company in town was terrific. The food was filling. But I'm so glad to be back on the PCT with Lone Star ahead of me.

She left the road and climbed the right-hand side of a long approach valley.

Hiking isn't as difficult as I expected. The next segment's twenty-six miles across the San Jacinto Mountains to the San Gorgonio Valley. My first substantial elevation gains and drops. I'm not worried.

At first, the sun burned her arms and she was thankful for the frequent shade offered by lichen-splotched boulders, prickly pear cacti, and tall brush. But an hour later when she stopped for lunch, a thick fog descended from the heights ahead and enveloped her. Before she finished eating, cold drizzle forced her into jacket and rain pants. A mile later, the once bright day degenerated into nasty gusts and raindrops the temperature of ice water. Another mile in, the sky was the color of slate. The path before her rose steeply onto the Desert Divide crest and into the unexpected storm.

By evening, the gale whipped hail and snow. Grace humped along, bent low like the wind-distorted firs around her. The narrow ridge afforded little protection. All she could do was lurch forward, one step at a time, into the maelstrom.

Hours earlier, a solo hiker had passed her, but he was nowhere in sight.

It's crazy cold.

Grace swallowed her fear.

The storm attacked first from one direction and then another, trying to knock her off her feet. Winds whistled eerily through the firs. Grace picked up her pace. In the increasing whiteout, even cacti became unrecognizable as their shapes morphed in the storm's deadly grip.

Icy roots pulled at her feet, threatening her balance.

"Okay, that does it. I'll set up my tent here. It's got to be safer than going on through this mess."

She pulled the nylon shelter from her pack. The tent poles whipped and beat her legs as she fitted them into the appropriate holes. The normally two-minute job defeated her numb, gloveless hands. With only one end of the tent standing, Grace thumped her ten fingers against her thighs.

Then a sudden gust seized the flapping material. She blinked. Her orange shelter whipsawed into a fir, billowed like a forgotten sail, and flew into the sky. The raging white closed around it.

My tent. Gone.

Grace's heart beat against her jacket.

What do I do now? I can't stay here. I'll freeze.

She tried to run. But all she could do was stumble through the punishing snow along the exposed ridge.

Keep going.

The trail ahead forked. One branch continued straight. Another dove into the relative shelter of a grove. Grace descended, head bowed. The trees were plastered glassy white. Her feet slid on the thin coating of ice.

She shivered uncontrollably.

Make a shelter. Where's my knife?

She clutched the one-inch blade between her palms and sliced at the nylon rope of her bear bag. After several attempts, she succeeded in tying the four corners of her ground cloth to surrounding trees, creating a protected area for her head. She laid out her waterproof bivy sack and stuffed her pad and sleeping bag inside. With the wind raging through the sparse trees, Grace zipped herself into her makeshift refuge.

Night fell. The storm's intensity increased.

How did I get myself into another Texas-sized mess? Without Lone Star.

The wind howled. Grace lay trembling in the mud, sleet, and hail.

CHAPTER 8

Grace pulled the sleeping bag over her head, trying to dampen the storm's screeching.

What kind of disaster magnet am I? What was I thinking last year when I came up with the brilliant idea of hiking the PCT alone?

***

"Who's that?" Celine's disheveled head appeared above the brown sofa when Grace entered Kenji's apartment six weeks after his death.

"Oh, Christ." Grace dropped her purse in surprise.

Celine tumbled off the couch. "I'm sorry I scared you."

"I scared you just as much." Grace caught her breath. *"What are you doing here? I thought the apartment was totally empty. I expected it to smell like a science experiment. Food rotting in the refrigerator. I was ready for the worst. Have you been here this whole time?"*

Celine looked at the floor.

"Come on." Grace pointed to the sofa. "Let's park ourselves. I think you're about to tell me a long story."

Celine and Grace faced each other on the soft leather. Grace shifted uneasily when Celine didn't speak. "I have to apologize, Celine. We exchanged numbers at the funeral. But I never called you like I said I would."

"Child, please. I have a finger to dial. I wasn't exactly leaving you a load of messages either." Celine paused.

Grace's eyes took her in.

She looks nothing like when I saw her then. Her cheeks are sunken. Her skin looks sickly without makeup. She's aged about ten years.

"Do you come here to think about Kenji?"

"I guess." Celine's hands played with the hem of her tank top. "You know..." She smoothed the legs of her jeans. "It's like he's still here when I'm here. Like he went to the store or something. Sometimes I lie here on the sofa all night, pretending he's going to come home." She sniffled.

"I know how you feel." Grace's fingers rubbed hard at an old coffee stain on the couch. "Say, I don't mean to change the subject, but what the heck is that music? Is it the same song over and over again, or am I imagining it?"

"No." Celine rubbed her nose with her sleeve. Her face wore a tender expression. "You're not. It's the same one. I played it for Kenji when we were getting dressed that afternoon. I always put songs on repeat. It used to drive him crazy." Celine stood

to get a tissue.

Grace's eyes wandered. She took in the bookcase between two windows facing a neighbor's house. Half the shelves were filled with Japanese manga, books on motorcycles, and a few physics and biology tomes. Books by Cheever and Dickens were interspersed randomly with ones by Phillis Wheately, Maya Angelou, and Jamaica Kincaid on the others.

Celine rejoined her on the couch. "That night at the party." Grace stopped and checked Celine's face for renewed evidence of tears. "Kenji talked about settling down with you. But you guys had already settled down, hadn't you? This is your apartment too, right?"

Celine's body stiffened as though she had been slapped. "I'm not trying to freeload. I know your parents are paying the rent. Kenji and I lived here together a lot of the time. But we hadn't told you guys yet. And see? I'm getting my stuff." She pointed to a few boxes in the corner of the room by the kitchen door. "I already started. I was going to pack up his stuff for you too. Clean this place. So you guys wouldn't have to do anything."

"Oh, Celine." Grace exhaled. "That's so hard. Too hard for you to do alone. Don't worry about the rent. The way my parents are acting, I don't think they'll be over here until sometime next decade. I think they want to keep this place as a shrine. This apartment's about as accessible to them right now as Antarctica."

Celine shrugged. "Well, I guess I'm doing the same thing. Keeping it as a shrine. Except I'm here, like, all the time. Praying he'll come back." She wiped away two tears that rolled down her cheeks and took a deep breath. *"I'm not breaking down again, don't worry."*

"It's okay. I don't know where my head is at these days either. I put my sunglasses in the freezer and frozen pizza in the top drawer of the dresser last night. Sometimes I wonder which way is up." She cocked her head toward the rest of the apartment. *"Why don't you give me a tour? We can both use the distraction."*

"Awesome. Well, this is the living room." Celine swept her arm around the room. Then she furrowed her eyebrows. *"Haven't you been here before?"*

"I have to admit it's been a while. I didn't even know you two were living together, remember?" Grace pointed at the bookshelf and some paintings. *"Those are yours, right?"*

"Yeah. I brought those over a few months ago." The blush as she said it brought needed color to her cheeks. *"I've still got my own apartment. I've got all my work clothes and stuff there. But on some week nights and all weekends..."*

"You came here. I understand." Grace jumped up. *"Show me what else you did."*

Celine led her to the kitchen. She paused, hand on the doorknob. *"Do you remember the awful wallpaper in here?"*

"Oh my god, yes. It was disgusting. Peeling and hanging down in strips. I always worried it was going to fall into Kenji's soup."

"Me too. So we spent two weekends stripping it and repainting. Kenji looked things up online. We

76

went to a little hardware store in town and bought the tools. The stuff's still in the hall closet. We said we were going to paint the bathroom next." Celine's arm drooped.

"You can always come fix up my place." Grace stepped past her, turned the knob, and entered. *"Wow."* She checked her stride and spun around. *"I'm serious. Let's make a date. You have to come over to my place if you can pull this off."*

The walls shone in the morning light with an iridescent yellow that multiplied each sunbeam twenty-fold. The cobalt blue window casements drew the eye. A coat of eggshell matte transformed the 1970s cabinets into art deco masterpieces.

"I feel like I'm in Greece." Grace whistled with admiration. *"Sun and water all around me."* She whirled. *"You work in a bank, right? You're not a professional decorator, right?"*

Celine chuckled, her features brightening. *"Straight up. I work at a computer behind a desk all day, advising folks on mortgages. Super fun. A superb use of my new college education. Filling out forms all day really taxes my grey cells."*

"All this wasted talent." Grace ran her fingers along the wall. *"How did you make it shimmer like this?"*

"Glitter topcoat. You put it on the base color. It's easy."

"For a professional, maybe. I'm into Japanese minimalist. It hides I have no style. You should see my place."

Celine's gaze dropped to the floor. *"I'd love to see it."*

Grace heard the disappointment in Celine's voice. "I am serious. I was an idiot for not calling you before. I should have invited you over. But I was too..."

"No, girl, you don't have to explain. We're all..."

"I know." The room suddenly felt too small and Grace walked over to the window and pulled the curtains aside. She tilted her head to look beyond the neighbor's grey siding and glimpse the blue sky. "It shouldn't be like that. My whole family's crawled into these individual holes in the ground. I know we have to grieve in our own ways, but I don't want to stay in a hole the rest of my life. I came here to get a little sunshine. And I'm glad I'm not alone."

"Me too."

The two women strolled around the apartment. Celine pointed out improvements: new faucets in the bathroom, a dimmer switch in the bedroom, paintings added to the walls. When they came to the second bedroom, Celine left her hand on the doorknob without turning it.

"I haven't actually gone in here before."

Grace lay her hand on the door carefully, as if she were afraid it might burn her. "Not at all? In all these weeks?"

"Nope."

"What's in there?"

"You'll see." Celine threw open the door and marched in with Grace on her heels. The bare hardwood floor was strewn with plastic tubs, each crammed with oddly-shaped contents. Cardboard

boxes and clothes lay scattered in a curiously organized way. Piles of colorfully filled baggies climbed the walls. Grace recognized jars of almond butter, cans of sardines, and packs of AA lithium batteries. In a corner she noticed clothing, hats, and what looked like a huge safari knife still in its original wrapping.

"I don't get it. Were you two selling stuff on Ebay?"

"No." Celine's eyes sparkled and she winked at Grace. "Guess again."

"Donating stuff for tsunami victims?"

"Not even close."

Grace took another look and discovered a scale similar to ones she'd seen at the post office. It occupied an honored location in the middle of the floor, surrounded by a clearing. "You were obviously weighing something. Aren't those labels near the boxes?"

"Yeah. And look over there." Celine pointed to a backpack hanging on a hook from the closet door. "That's a hint."

Grace picked her way across the room to the sack of green and black nylon. It lacked fancy zippers or straps. Her fingers felt the material. "I've never seen a pack like this before. Looks basically like a duffle bag. I give up."

"It's for hiking."

A growing awareness grew in Grace's chest. She glanced around again. "All this is for hiking? Where was he going? Nepal?"

"Nope. Canada."

Her foot nudged a bag of dried beans. "They

don't have food in Canada?"

Celine snickered. "He wasn't starting in Canada. That's where the route ends. He was going to hike the Pacific Crest Trail. It starts at the Mexican border and goes through California, Oregon, and Washington."

"So which part was he going to hike?"

"All of it."

"You're kidding. How long does that take? Years?"

"About five months."

"You're serious?"

"Absolutely."

"That's nuts."

"Absolutely." Celine returned Grace's long stare.

Without another word, they returned to the living room.

"So, Kenji was going to hike from Mexico to Canada?" Grace rolled her eyes. "That's what he was talking about at the party?"

"That was the plan. He spent all his free time arranging things. He was in that room a lot. Always obsessing about details. Weighing everything. Scared he wasn't taking the right stuff. Worried he'd get sick of the food he'd picked out."

"And what about all the cardboard boxes? I don't get that."

"They're drop boxes. Boxes I was going to send him."

"Huh?" Grace pushed hair from her face. "How would he get the boxes if he was out in the middle of the wilderness?"

"He'd hitchhike or walk into towns with post offices. You send stuff there and they hold it for you until you pick it up. We printed out labels from the PCT Website."

"PCT? You mean the Pacific Whatever Trail?"

"Crest. And I can't believe I'm sounding like a fricking expert. I know jack. Just what Kenji told me."

"When he said at the picnic he was going hiking, I thought he meant an overnight trip. You know, sneaking into Muir Woods to sleep under the redwoods like we did when we were kids. Maybe a week in Yosemite. But what you're describing sounds like a full-time job."

Celine nodded. "More like a full-time adventure."

"What'd he think he'd get out of it?"

"At night he'd say, 'Celine, I found part of myself when I found you. Now I have to find the other part.'" Celine's voice faltered.

Grace leaned across the sofa and gave the young woman a squeeze.

"Look, Celine. I know you want him back. So do I. But I don't think it's good for you to be here by yourself every weekend. This isn't a shrine. More like a tomb. And you're too young and pretty to turn into a zombie. Let's plan on coming here together next Saturday. I can help you do a little packing, okay?"

That evening, Grace pulled a wooden kitchen chair into her one-bedroom condominium's bay window. She sat in the dark, staring out at the blackness of San Rafael Bay in the distance.

If Kenji were hiking, he could walk from here to San Francisco. Or from here to Sacramento. Or to Oregon. He could walk to Canada. So what about me?

***

A few days later, Grace and her sister sat in a bright Vietnamese restaurant in Oakland.

"Did I tell you Harrison got a job offer in Atlanta?" Hope bit into a vermicelli summer roll.

Grace choked on her iced coffee. "What? Atlanta? No, you didn't tell me. I'd remember something like that." Her complexion blanched and then regained its color. "Oh, wait. You're kidding. Very funny, Hope. You had me there for a moment." She grinned and attacked her noodle dish.

Hope didn't speak. Grace raised her head. Then she dropped her chopsticks. They bounced off her bowl and clattered to the floor, rolling across the pink and grey linoleum to the neighboring table.

Hope picked them up, wrapped them in her napkin, and placed them with exaggerated care alongside her plate.

"Hope." Grace flicked her finger insistently against her water glass. "Look at me. Your husband didn't get a job offer on the East Coast, right? You're not going to move, are you?"

Hope pantomimed to a waitress that Grace needed another pair of chopsticks.

Grace knocked the hot sauce container against the table. "Look at me, Hope." Hope raised her eyes. "This has to be a joke."

"Grace, it's not that bad. I didn't just tell you I had cancer. Atlanta's still in the United States." Hope waited. But Grace refused to look at her. *"I'm sorry I didn't tell you before. Nothing's firm yet. Harrison flew out two weeks ago for an interview. He got the call yesterday. It's still being negotiated. He wants more money than they're offering."*

Grace snorted.

"I know you don't like Harrison. But he's trying to do his best for us."

"Like the way he always forgets his wallet when we go out to dinner, so that I have to pay?" As soon as the words were out of her mouth, Grace shot her arm across the table. *"Oh, Hope. I didn't mean that."* She took a deep breath and rubbed her crumpled napkin hard against her lips. *"It's Kenj."* Her words filtered through falling bits of paper.

"I know. Now it's always Kenji. Even if we're talking about the Wi-Fi being slow or the windows needing cleaning. I can't get away from him. At the same time, I never want to stop thinking about him." Hope ran her hand through her thick bob, as though trying to wipe away a memory. Her shoulders sagged. *"What should I do?"*

"Please stay. I need my little sister."

"I can't promise, Grace. I've got two kids. And our family's falling apart."

"You and Harrison?"

"No. Us. You and me. Mom and Dad. It's all such a mess now. I used to hate going to Mom and Dad's on Sundays. They were always fussing over Kenji. Sometimes I thought they wouldn't even notice if the rest of us didn't show up. Now I would

give anything to do it one more time."

Grace reached for Hope's hands and spoke slowly, with a pause between each word. "I want you to stay near me, Hope. But that's what I want. You have to do what you want."

After lunch, outside the restaurant, she returned to the subject. "Keep Harrison's job offer a secret until things are clearer, okay? The last thing we need is Mom going ballistic because her daughter's moving across the country. Or that she crashes into some kind of depression. You never know with her. She's like the stock market—hard to predict."

"I won't say anything until it's firm."

"Good. Mom and Dad both seem so brittle."

Or maybe, *Grace thought two weeks later,* that was how I felt.

Her mother and she stood in the Mori family kitchen. Grace scooped fried rice and garlic shrimp from takeout containers onto plates.

Her mother's high-pitched Japanese broke the silence. "Dad and I want to move back home to Japan."

Grace dropped the box. Two shrimp caught in her blouse. Her mother sighed, pulled Grace's arm over the sink, and shook the sleeve vigorously. The renegade prawns plopped onto stainless steel and slithered into the disposal.

"Sit down." She led Grace to a chair. "You want some tea?" She pumped a thermos pot. Hot water filled a delicate clay bowl. She swirled the tea around and poured Grace a small cupful.

Grace pushed the cup away. "You are moving back to Japan." Her Japanese was slow and careful. "After all these years?"

Her mother stood beside her, hands cupping the tea bowl. "Do not worry. We will not go soon. But with Kenji gone, nobody needs us anymore. You have your job. Hope has her family. We think we could have a second beginning back home in Japan. A second spring."

Grace's accusing eyes sought her mother's. "I thought this was your home." Her finger pointed around the room.

"It is. But we want to go back to where we came from. Where we really belong."

"You do not belong here? What about Dad's job?"

"He can retire. He has been thinking about it for years."

Grace felt dizzy.

Thirty-three years in this family, and I still don't know what's going on half the time.

"Mom. I thought we all had to stay together." The words caught in her throat.

Her mother patted her shoulders. "America has 9-11. The Moris have 4-14. You cannot change that, Grace. Kenji is gone. And from the point we lost him, everything was different."

A small puff of air escaped Grace's lips, half sigh, half assent.

"I hope you never know what it is like to lose a child. I would do anything in the world to get him back. Sometimes I feel so sad I think my ribs will crack open. My heart will fall on the floor. But then I remember I still have you and Hope. That gives me the strength to go on."

"I did not know you feel that way. I guess I cannot really imagine."

"Dad and I will take things slowly. But in the end, we all have to figure out how to move on."

On her drive home, phrases reverberated in Grace's head, bouncing off each other, loud and distorted. Moving. Where we belong. A second beginning. *To distract herself, she called Celine at a stop light.*

Her fingers drummed the steering wheel while she waited for Celine to pick up. "Celine? It's Grace. This family's too crazy."

"What? Where you at, Grace?"

"In the car. Long story. I'll tell you when I see you. Have you been to Kenji's yet this weekend?"

"No, girl. I was waiting for you to call."

"Want to meet me there now?"

"Now? Okay. I'll be there in ten."

"It'll take me more like twenty. I'll be there as soon as I can."

Move on. That's what I told Ben I needed to do when we split up. Now everyone in my family seems to have gotten that message but me.

When Grace arrived at Kenji's, Celine sat on the living room floor, packing her side of the bookshelf into sturdy boxes. A happy pop song played.

"Thought I'd start on some stuff." Another book flew into the box. *"It's weird, but this is the first time I'm doing this without bawling my eyes out."*

"Funny how what they say is true." Grace *tossed her purse over the back of the couch.*

"What do you mean?"

"Time heals all wounds." Grace *dropped to the*

floor and leaned against the sofa. "I think everyone but me is confronting what happened."

"I don't know about that. You're the one who came over here first. And you can get me started crying again real easy. But tonight I feel like being happy again." Celine shrugged her shoulders. "I finally changed the playlist on the iPod."

"I thought this music was different." Grace watched Celine pack books for a few minutes in silence. "Do you have any more of those boxes?" She pushed herself to her feet.

"Got a ton in my trunk. I've been carting them around, like, forever."

"Can I have your keys? I'm going to start packing that stuff in the other bedroom, okay?"

Celine reached in the pocket of her jeans and threw Grace the set. "You go, girl."

An hour later, Celine came into the bedroom where Grace knelt on the floor next to one packed box.

"Wanted to see how you're doing." Celine pushed the box to the side and sat down. "You don't seem to have gotten far."

Grace picked items one by one from the plastic containers surrounding them. There were tubs of pretzels, packages of M&Ms, and Snickers bars. Tuna and salmon in resealable pouches. Identical-looking white packets that had Pasta Roni, Rice-A-Roni, oatmeal, *and* instant mashed potatoes *scribbled on them in red magic marker. Plastic baggies of raisins and banana chips. She raised a bag.*

"Fish food?"

"Nope. Textured vegetable protein."

She flung another at Celine. "Cocaine?"

"Funny." Celine lobbed it back at her. *"That's breakfast shake mix."*

Grace turned over a bin, letting the contents tumble to the foor. "I didn't even know Kenji liked half this stuff."

Celine's careful fingers replaced the items one by one. "Be happy you didn't live with him. I had to try everything. Instant mashed potatoes with tuna mixed in for five days straight."

"Why on earth?"

"To see if he could stand it. To see how long it took to cook. I have to say, some of the stuff was nasty. Like this." She held up a bag labeled corn pasta. *"I told him I'd rather starve than eat this again."*

Grace looked as though she were struggling with a difficult algebra problem. "Why aren't there any canned foods? Or some of those hiker freeze-dried things?"

"Too heavy or too expensive. All this," Celine encompassed the room with a sweep of her arm, *"cost about a thousand bucks. It took him six months to weigh it all and decide what to eat when. See?"*

She pointed to a masking tape label on one of the boxes. "The boxes all have numbers. He made a list. It's here somewhere." Celine rummaged through a container of maps and other papers. *"Here it is."* She handed Grace an Excel printout of each box's contents, weight, and destination.

"What a waste." Grace let the printout drop. *"I*

guess I can give the food to a shelter."

Celine shook her head. "Already asked at work. A girl there volunteers downtown. They'll take the stuff that's in glass or a can, but it has to be in the original packaging. And most of this stuff isn't."

Grace surveyed the room again.

Enough meals and snacks to last for five months. Expensive clothing and equipment.

She walked to the closet and lifted the green and black backpack. It weighed next to nothing.

She slid her shoulders under the straps and fitted the waist belt around her middle. She looked at herself in the door mirror, pushing her long, highlighted hair out of the way.

"You can't be thinking what I think you're thinking."

Grace undid the belt clasp.

It's crazy, but it feels right. I was looking for a way to move on. Maybe this is it?

She shrugged her shoulders out of the straps and hung the pack on the door.

"I can see what you're thinking." Celine's voice took on the tone of a mother warding off a tantrum. "But that's five months of hiking. And you don't hike, do you?"

"I used to mountain bike. We all did. It was too tempting, with Mount Tam practically right outside our door. Mom used to make us wear helmets. Totally embarrassing at that point in life. I dumped mine by a tree on the way up and put it on again before riding home."

"But that was a long time ago, right? And a few bike rides aren't the same as hiking for months on

end."

"I know." Grace nudged a pair of hiking boots across the floor with her sandal.

"You want to hike the PCT?"

"Only if you'll help me." Grace faced the younger woman, who still sat on the floor. "I'd need somebody to drop off all those boxes and stuff."

"Grace, no offense, but you don't know the limits of your own ignorance. You don't drop the boxes off at the stops. You take them to the post office. The US government does the rest. The things you don't know would fill a book."

"Well, Kenji was counting on you to help him, right?"

"Yep. He was."

"So you'd help me too?"

"You don't know what you're asking. I'm ready to help. But the PCT is serious business." Celine stretched her slender legs and stood. "Come with me." She pointed toward the living room.

She walked to the now half-empty bookshelf and squatted to look at Kenji's side.

"Here." Celine hefted three thick, heavily worn paperback books from the shelf and handed them to Grace.

"What the heck are these? They weigh a ton." Grace read the spines. "Pacific Crest Trail guides. Have you read these?"

"Are you kidding?" Celine's nose crinkled. "I never touched them. But Kenji was on them like white on rice. He called them his PCT bibles. So I think you should take a good long look at them."

"Okay." Grace flipped through the pages of photos and maps. "I'll read them."

"Take your time."

"Well, honestly, I don't know if I'll have enough time to get through it all. Because if I decide to go, I'll be going soon."

"No, you won't."

Grace's mouth puckered into a pout. "Yes, I will. I don't want to wait."

"You're gonna have to wait, girl." Celine stood with her hands on her hips, the image of a schoolteacher reprimanding a rambunctious pupil.

"Why? Doing Kenji's hike will give me something I've been looking for. Waiting's not an option."

Celine shook her head. "Well, actually, it's your only option. Nobody starts the PCT in late June. Five months from then is well into winter. You'd be snowed in before you made it to Canada. You have to start before the desert heat gets too intense. And you have to end before the snow. That's why people start near Mexico around the end of April. There's some kind of meeting down there then. The Send Off, or something. Anyway, Kenji was going."

"I can't go now?"

"No way, José." Celine folded her arms and spread her feet apart. Then she shrugged. "Hey, look, who am I to tell you what to do? You're the psychologist. But this whole thing is a mother effin' crazy idea. And wanting to start now doesn't make it sound more sane."

As Grace drove home later, the three massive books slid aimlessly on the passenger seat.

Hope's thinking about moving to Atlanta. Our parents are moving back to Japan. Celine's playing happy music again. I'm not going to be the one who's stuck, glued to the same place I am today. Single. Lonely. Without a clear purpose. Kenji's hike, no matter how crazy, is my answer.

***

On the ridge, Grace shivered with fear and cold as a strong gust from the storm shook her bivy. She burrowed deeper into her sleeping bag.

Back then everything—the pack, the food, the boots—felt right. But I had absolutely no idea what I was getting myself into.

CHAPTER 9

At the same time as Grace marched unawares on the trail toward the blizzard at the top of the Desert Divide, a different storm of sorts was gathering much farther south.

At Lake Morena County Park near the Mexican border, almost five hundred wannabe thru-hikers assembled for the annual Day Zero Pacific Crest Trail Kick Off, known in the PCT hiking world as simply the Kick Off.

Experienced backpackers, complete novices, and all in between congregated for three days to socialize, prepare, and reminisce. Most were young, some had grey hair and wrinkles, and a few represented the middle age cohort. Overall, about a third were women.

Successful PCT end-to-enders from previous seasons returned to the Kick Off for the nostalgia, while rookies took the opportunity to gather valuable last-minute information about water caches, trail angels, gear, food, first aid, bears, and cell phone reception. Several hikers who started the trail earlier hitchhiked back to participate in the festivities. By day, people poked through vendors' displays of tents, hats, and packs. They attended lectures. Made new friends. At night, campfires provided the backdrop for camaraderie and song.

Hikers referred to this mass of northbound thrus as "the herd," a group of disparate souls united by love of the PCT. Some hopefuls would not survive the initial twenty, waterless miles. But at the Kick Off, all struggles still lay ahead. A NASA scientist, three dot com millionaires, sixteen ministers, thirty-eight camp counselors, and fifty-four marathon runners were among the hundreds gathered. Five had their pilot's license. Two had served time.

One had almost killed a girl. And one didn't care at all about the trail, only about revenge.

The majority of thrus took hiking seriously. But the lure of continuous partying drew a small number. These young, strong, mostly male hikers prepared for the weeks ahead by funneling vodka, gin, and rum into their water containers, concealing marijuana and other drugs in the small pockets of their packs, and drinking as much beer as possible while it was still readily available. Pulling down big miles to get to Canada interested them far less than hiking quickly to hit as many bars as possible along the way. Ultimately, if they ended their hike at Lake Tahoe, that wasn't going to be so bad, they thought.

After leaving the scene of his bicycle accident, fleeing Oakland, and spending months couch surfing in LA, Jerry Kriebel was attracted by this party group. The novelty of LA's punk music scene had worn off after repeated ejections for smuggling beer into arenas. Under-the-counter jobs paid for food, but Jerry resented cutting other people's lawns, cleaning other people's pools, and picking other people's fruit. Then one of his acquaintances mentioned the PCT.

"I did it last year. It was a total blast. Walked from Mexico straight north. Got hammered at bars on the way. Then I stopped at Tahoe for the rest of the summer and never looked back, man."

Jerry worried about the expense.

"Shit, you don't even have to buy any food. You beg from the serious hikers and go through what they leave behind. It's called 'yogi-ing'—don't ask me why. But these rich dudes always have too much stuff. It's crazy. They spend thousands of bucks on freeze-dried crap, and then they dump it because it weighs too much."

Jerry wondered about the gear.

"I'll give you mine. Who needs it in LA? I've even got a Bowie knife. All you'll have to get is shoes. And whatever keeps you flying high. Seriously, I never had so much fun. It's mostly guys, but if you aren't too picky, you can get some as you go along. The chicks are super horny after weeks without action. They never even know your real name, 'cause you make up a funny trail name and everybody uses that. So no knocked up girl's ever gonna find you."

Jerry's lips tightened into a knowing leer. "Action's what I'm good at. Screw foreplay and pillow talk. Doing it standing up against a tree suits me fine. So, how much is admission?"

"Just show up, dude. The last weekend of April

at Lake Morena County Park in Campo. Due east of San Diego. Got your driver's license back?"

"No."

"I'll give you a lift. Hell, I'll stay the weekend myself." The youth nudged Jerry. "Who knows? Maybe I'll find a hot girl looking for a trail veteran to show her the ropes."

The weekend of the Kick Off, a royal blue lowrider Chevy screeched to a stop in the campground lot early Friday afternoon. Jerry opened the door. Desert heat slapped him in the face and the pounding sunshine hammered him speechless.

"I don't know about this." He leaned his hand against the car then snatched it back. "Ow. That's fucking hot." But his concerns evaporated when his friend clapped him on the shoulder and pointed to a group of young women sitting under a tree, clad in floppy hats, zip-off pants, and nylon tops. None of them wore a bra.

"Okay. You convinced me." Jerry, grinning from ear to ear, walked up to say hello.

On a picnic table at the other end of the campground sat Ed Galeano, a thin, bedraggled man in camo. His hunched shoulders, creased brow, and deep frown made him look at least a decade older than his twenty-eight years. He had arrived at Lake Morena by bus, having ridden public transportation first from Oakland to LA, then LA to San Diego, and finally from San Diego to Campo. Three long, hot rides.

Ed surveyed the crowd from behind dark aviator sunglasses, wiping perspiration from his brow now and then before it dripped into his eyes. His thick long-sleeved shirt soaked up the sun in equal proportion to his sweat, and dark patches emphasized his underarms and back.

At Lake Morena, Ed's disheveled appearance blended in with the crowd of thrus. A few hikers approached him as he sat on the picnic table and invited him to the lunch being dished out under a makeshift tarp. Ed declined.

"I like it where I am. I can see all the people in the chow line."

A slight breeze rippled his short-cropped hair. He remained absorbed by the queue. Crowds of hikers edged toward the servers. The group moved slowly.

Ed's fists clenched and unclenched as he scanned the faces.

Then his eyes focused. A laughing, shirtless man, back half-turned to Ed, greeted a young woman. The man nudged his neighbor in the ribs and offered the woman a beer from a cooler. The pretty brunette shook her head, shoved his outstretched hand away, and left the line. The man shrugged and turned to the food, exposing a snake tattoo that crawled across his bare chest.

Ed tensed.

After a minute of watching the man, he hopped off the table and stalked toward the campground. He marched around empty tents, guy-lines, and backpacks until a hidden stake snagged his boot. He untangled it, cursing.

Then he wiped his face with his sleeve and stood erect.

"I don't have to do anything now," he said under his breath as he picked his way back to the picnic through the colorful assortment of gear. "There's only one trail. I have from here to Canada to find him alone. I'll watch and wait. And when I get him, I'll bring him to his knees. He'll pay for what he did to my life."

Ed joined the end of the lunch line. He chatted casually with the hikers around him as he heaped his plate with hot dogs and beans and covertly scanned the grassy area where hundreds of hungry thrus clumped in small groups to eat one of their last easy meals.

His eyes caught those of someone who'd approached him earlier. The man waved and Ed joined his group on the sandy ground, his back to where Jerry caroused with a cluster of young men around a keg.

The man shook Ed's hand. "So, are you ready for the thru-hike?"

"I'm prepared." Ed glanced at the assembled crowd. "But I bet some people aren't. Nasty things can happen on the trail."

CHAPTER 10

Later that night, much farther north, the mountain-top blizzard raged around Grace's emergency shelter. Trees moaned and creaked with each ferocious gust. Now and again branches gave way under the weight of ice and snow, shaking the ground. Grace poked the tarp overhead to rid it of accumulation. When the wind abated toward morning, she finally fell asleep.

Well after dawn, Grace crawled from her refuge into mud and slush. A startlingly blue sky glowed against snow and ice-covered firs that dwarfed her jerry-rigged tarp. Her pack lay bespattered with mud and ice beneath its ripstop nylon cover.

I made it. San Francisco-size woman lives through Texas-size storm.

Her sleeping bag was a collection of sodden down clumps. Grace spread it out to dry and sat in the welcome sunshine.

Keep hiking? Or quit while I'm still alive?

The woods around her seemed made of glass, startlingly bright, clear, and brittle. Icicles dripped in the morning light. Branches sparkled and creaked. Snow fluttered on the remaining breeze.

Back to town. I'll make up my mind there. I need convincing that hiking alone isn't a suicidal plan.

She hefted her pack to rejoin the PCT and head south, toward Idyllwild.

How much farther ahead is Lone Star going to get now? At this rate, the only way to catch him is going to be in a car.

At the Pines to Palms Highway, she stood for half an hour as a trickle of vehicles passed her outstretched thumb. Finally, a navy minivan rolled to a stop.

"My daughters are all girl scouts." The middle-aged woman in the driver's seat pushed a button and the van door closed softly behind Grace, enveloping her in the scents of potato chips, ice cream, and gum. "I have a soft spot for female hikers."

Grace perched on the middle row amid soccer balls, dog leashes, and half-empty soda bottles. Her driver concentrated on the road. Grace pulled her cell phone from its Ziploc baggie and scrolled through recent pictures until she found the photo of Lone Star's last hiker register note.

In his characteristic slanting script it read:

Darling Just Grace,

You must be getting used to trail life by now. You've probably had some more adventures—got my fingers crossed they're all Rhode Island-size. I hope in between you're enjoying the views, the sunrises, and the sunsets.

I'm busy as a hound in flea season trying to beat the herd. I'm sure they'll catch up with me eventually, but I'm quick out of the chute. Still, the experience of hiking alone has never been so difficult before. No getting around it. I miss you more than all get-out. I've been working on that poem. Here's the next stanza.

> *I worried so about you there.*
> *My heart was drawn with fear.*
> *Your breath so quick your eyes so clear,*
> *The time was ours to share.*
> *Thinking of you lots and lots...and lots,*
> *Lone Star*

Grace sighed and put the phone away.

If Lone Star had been there last night, he would have seen that storm coming. I thought I was pretty good at predicting the weather. I've been out on the trail for weeks already. But I obviously know nothing about the mountains.

If I could only talk to him. Why did I pick the only person out here whose fanciest electrical device is a headlamp?

I could rent a car. Drive to the next place the PCT crosses a road. Sit there until those size fourteen hiking shoes came along. I don't have to keep hiking. Nobody's got a knife to my throat.

In town, she chose a room with a balcony that overlooked central Idyllwild and spent the next days searching her mind about what to do next.

"Are you hiking the PCT?" On Grace's third evening in a row, the same motherly waitress in a frilly white apron brought her the check. "Sorry if I'm being nosy."

Grace blinked with surprise. "What makes you ask?"

"I always know when a hiker's sitting at my table. They eat more than two regular customers combined. Wish I could do that and get away with it." The woman patted her ample middle.

Grace fished her credit card out of a Ziploc bag. "I'm actually thinking of quitting the trail. So if I keep eating like this, I'll probably gain fifty pounds."

The woman shook her head. "You won't quit. I've never seen a sadder face than that of a hiker who has to quit. And you don't look sad."

"Maybe. But I'm not sure what I'm going to do. I had a little scare out there."

The woman swept the check and card into her apron and stacked Grace's dishes. "Keep hiking. You can always quit later."

"I guess."

"Take it from me." She hoisted the large pyramid of plates onto one forearm. "I've seen hundreds of thrus. Maybe thousands. Quitting doesn't solve your problems."

Grace fidgeted on the seat. "What if hiking's my

problem?"

"If hiking was your problem, you wouldn't have made it to Idyllwild."

A smile poked at the corners of Grace's mouth. "What do I owe you for the psychotherapy?"

The waitress grinned. "Just leave me a big tip."

The next afternoon, Grace threw herself on the mercy of the town's outdoor supplies store salesman. "I'm hiking the PCT. I lost my tent in a storm. Do you know anything about tents?"

"Was Moses Jewish?" The man's accent placed him as a native of somewhere east of the Hudson River. "I hiked the PCT ten years ago and haven't left California since. I love helping thrus." He took in Grace's enormous pack. "Especially novices. Can I go through your stuff to give you some advice?"

Grace laid her pack in front of him. He tipped it over and its contents cascaded onto the linoleum floor.

"Your cooking pot weighs a ton. You don't need both a headlamp and a flashlight. Your sleeping bag's shot." He peered at her over thick reading glasses. "You've got serious climbing ahead of you. Let's see what we can do to shave off a few ounces. In addition to all the rest of it, your stove's too heavy, *capisce*? Why carry all that propane? What you need is a pop can stove."

He retreated to the storage area and emerged with the remains of a folded Mountain Dew can. "I'll let you have this for nothing. Buy some denatured alcohol and you'll be set. I'll show you how to use it when we're done."

"Done with what? My brother spent months

getting ready for the PCT. I'm using most of his stuff. I thought I *was* set."

"Set if you're planning on having a Sherpa carry this." He tossed aside rain pants, sun hat, water filter, dishes, utensil set, and towel. He tried to discard her San Diego County Parks and Recreation bottle, but Grace yelped. She clutched it to her chest as she watched.

"I actually worked hard on getting my weight down before I started." Kenji's down jacket flew onto the increasing mound.

"If you don't have the right gear, you'll suffer the whole way. You might even quit." The clerk looked up at her from his knees. "You don't want to quit, do you?"

Grace shook her head. "Go on. I know I need help."

"What's this?" Kenji's apartment key dangled from the zipper of Grace's first aid kit.

"My first aid kit."

"I mean this." The clerk flicked the key with his middle finger. "Extra ounces. This is exactly the kind of thing I'm talking about." He fiddled with the twist tie that secured the key.

Grace snatched the kit away from him. "I need that. It's…well, it's like a good luck charm."

The man shrugged his shoulders. "Suit yourself. But get rid of the kit. All you need is a few gauze pads, a bandage roll, and a sling. I've got some sets made up at the counter."

"Thanks. But I think I'll keep the whole kit. To be on the safe side. I'm a little accident prone."

After an hour of strategic shopping, Grace asked

him to weigh her old equipment against her new. He nodded with intense satisfaction. "Guess how much weight I saved you?"

Grace stared at the new items. "A pound?"

"Naw. Not even warm. Guess again."

"Five pounds?"

"I saved you eight pounds, thirteen ounces. That's including the tent."

Grace pumped his hand and then closed her eyes when she signed the credit card receipt.

That night as she lay in her hotel bed, Grace composed a poem of her own.

Dearest Lone Star,
The sun is blazing from the sky.
Again it's only me and I.
I wish I could share my water with you,
And not just my water but something else too.
My heart is beating faster now.
I think of seeing you again, but how?
Are we going to come together? When?
I won't let you go so soon again then.
Just wait till I get my arms around you,
Grace

The next morning, she hiked the path from the Pines-to-Palms Highway for the third time in less than a week. The base weight of her pack, the weight without food, water, or fuel, had gone from over thirty-seven pounds to under twenty-eight.

My posture's better. My step's secure. I can do

this for a few days longer. Maybe even catch up a bit.

And then she met the first hikers from the herd.

Grace heard them before she saw them. Footsteps pounded the trail behind her at twice her normal rate. Young thrus passed her with an effortless, loping gait and had little time for chitchat.

They zoomed the one hundred fifty miles from the Kick Off in less than five days. Thirty or more miles per day. Their packs are miniscule. They didn't even stop at Idyllwild.

Another thru whizzed by.

I thought I'd picked up my pace. But these guys are running to Canada. How's that even possible?

Some passed Grace at a more leisurely pace and relayed rumors of what happened elsewhere on the trail. They helped her analyze past storms, and predict future ones. They discussed snow levels in the mountains ahead. Shared where trail angels had supplied an additional water cache, how to detour around a bridge that washed away in a flash flood, and the containment status of a wildfire near the trail. It was her first taste of the PCT's grapevine.

"This guy had to be helicoptered out because he fell off a cliff while hiking. I didn't see it, but I heard it was amazing. They said the helicopter's dust cloud could be seen for miles."

Or, "You know how when you're in Yellowstone and there's one car parked by the side of the road? And then all these other cars start pulling over 'cause the people think someone spotted some amazing wild animal? Well, right when the herd was starting out at Campo, there was this guy bent over looking for something. Soon there were, like, fifty thrus all bent over, digging in the sand. Crazy. Turns out he was looking for one lousy M&M."

And, "This year's PCT party group gave themselves alcohol trail names. Bud, Gordon, Stoli, Ecstasy, Southern Comfort, Bacardi, and Margie. Margie's short for Margaritaville. I got a look at Margie before I took off. Between you and me, I would *love* to search for her lost shaker of salt."

That first evening back on the trail, the orange glow faded from the horizon over Little Tahquitz Valley as a young couple from upstate New York, Chow Hound and Teva, joined Grace. This was their second thru-hike, they said. They had hiked the Appalachian Trail together the summer before, beginning the day after their engagement.

"That seems like a rough start."

"Not really." Teva draped her socks over her dusty shoes and stretched her toes. "We were counselors at a wilderness camp. Our kids were not exactly little angels. They were always fighting with kitchen knives and burning down tents and running away. It was kind of like working at an outdoor detention facility. So when we got out on the AT, we kept saying how quiet and peaceful everything was."

"Then it's too bad you weren't here a few nights ago. A big storm went through. It was anything but peaceful. I've never been so scared in my life. I would have loved some company. I wouldn't have been picky. An escaped convict or two would have been welcome. Plus it was freezing. I wasn't sure whether I was going to die from being hit by a falling tree or from hypothermia."

"Sorry we missed it." Teva leaned against her husband. "Chow Hound here never gets cold. But me? I'm always shivering. That's why we share a sleeping bag. So I can cool him down and he can warm me up." Chow Hound handed Teva a power bar and she munched it in the increasing darkness. "So, what brought you out here all by yourself?"

Grace hesitated. "I haven't made up my mind yet. I thought I was doing this for my brother. He wanted to hike the PCT. But...well...he can't now. So I guess I'm hiking to figure out what to do with my life. It also sort of feels like a survival odyssey."

"Because you have to eat the same food day in and day out?" Teva held up a stuff sack bulging with rectangles. "Chow Hound and I let ourselves get hungry. That way power bars taste better." She smiled, shrugged, and ripped open her second. "It saves weight, not having to cook anything. But that's not what you're talking about."

Grace shook her head. "No. I'm getting used to the food. It's more about not having people around to talk to. Or going through something like that storm. By myself. Then I wonder why I'm not back in my comfortable office in San Francisco. Knowing what to expect every day. Back there I have friends. Out here I meet people I like and then they disappear. Like you guys. It's great to sit around tonight, but I'm sure you'll be gone in the morning. I'm not complaining. And, obviously, I haven't quit yet..." Grace trailed off.

Chow Hound and Teva exchanged a look. Chow

Hound excused himself and began setting up their tent at a sociable distance. Teva watched him clear the area of stones, twigs, and other debris. Then she scooted closer to Grace.

"I know how you feel. Chow Hound wanted to give me the trail name Cry Baby when we started the AT. I was always crying about the same things you're talking about. I missed my family. I was scared. I had blisters and my muscles ached. I didn't feel like we'd made a good decision. My parents argued we should save our money and go to Puerto Rico for the honeymoon, and those first weeks I was pretty sure they were right. I wasn't exactly the best hiking partner, I can tell you. But after about a month, I got to the point where life felt okay the way it was."

"I'm not sure I get that."

Teva dug in the bag for another bar. "I mean, after a while, you stop worrying about the past or the future. You're happy where you are right now. If you're alone—and I had some time alone because Chow Hound's mom got real sick, and he had to leave the trail for a few weeks—then you're happy being alone. If it rains, it rains. If things are hard, then they're hard. They're not sucky or miserable. They're just hard."

She glanced at Grace. "I don't know if I can explain it, but I guess I'd say tough it out for a couple weeks longer. If you feel what I'm talking about, you'll know it. You'll be happy where you are. Life will get brighter and more exciting, no matter if you're sitting on a rock facing the bottom of a mountain wall or you're on top of a ridge and the world is at your feet. You'll be a thru, not someone out for a walk. Life will feel different."

Teva and Chow Hound were gone when Grace awoke the next morning. But a power bar lay tucked inside one of Grace's boots.

Lone Star's ahead. Maybe even waiting for me. I can do a couple more weeks. How hard can that be?

CHAPTER 11

Far south of Grace's camp, the bulk of the herd made its way north.

Most PCT thrus began at the Mexican border within the same fourteen-day period. Some, like those passing Grace, almost flew up the trail, while others found the conditions too challenging to walk more than ten miles per day. The relentless sun and heat culled a few from the group permanently. Those who persevered soon found their own pace, fast or slow. Leapfrogging was common, as one hiker passed another only to be caught by that same person hours, days, or weeks later.

Most hikers spent at least part of every day alone on the trail. Jerry Kriebel, the young man with the snake tattoo, was an exception. At the Kick Off, he attached himself to a group of six compatriots for whom hiking was something to do between parties. They stuck together like ice cubes in a glass. Jerry had no hiking experience, but weeks of walking toned even his apathetic muscles.

Ed Galeano trailed behind the hard-drinking

group, unable to single Jerry out and growing increasingly frustrated. Blisters plagued his feet. His back ached from the weight of his Army surplus pack. His skin burned in the sun. But he tracked his prey relentlessly. A dull rage pounded in his chest from before dawn to the time he crawled into his camouflage sleeping bag at night.

"Why the fuck are they together all the time?" He addressed the cacti as he walked along.

Amid sandy hills and dusty brush, the scent of the group's marijuana often lingered in the hot desert air. Rowdy shouts from their camp reverberated for miles. Ed hunched in his solitary shelter under a thousand stars and cursed.

"I'm suffering while he's getting high. Someday soon, I'll make him pay."

Ed kept himself company for the long hours of hiking with a repetitive monologue. "I had a good life before that scumbag came along. I was going somewhere. I owned a store. I liked my job. Then the bike accident, that little girl, and everybody thought I did it. My life went down the tubes. It was all Jerry's fault. And now he's out here having the time of his life. Like nothing ever happened"

Ed kicked hard at the dirt in the trail, launching stones and other debris high into the air.

"I could smash his face into a cactus. Or bury him up to his neck in sand, leave him to dry in the sun, and come back to find his body shriveled like a discarded snake skin. I could poison his water supply. Or push him down an icy mountainside and watch him roll, flip, and bump until he's a speck at the bottom of a mile-long crevasse."

He picked up a rock and threw it at the pinprick on the horizon that was Jerry and his friends.

"I could do anything. If I caught him alone. I went down for the crime *he* committed. But I'm not going down for the one *I* commit. No fucking witness this time."

With each sweltering mile of the PCT, Ed's furor intensified. His target remained as unconcerned as a savanna warthog being stalked by a silent leopard.

***

Two weeks after the Kick Off, in the middle of May, the large mass of the herd surrounded Grace.

I'm hiking like a tortoise with an oil drum on its back. Or whatever Lone Star would say. I can't afford to fall farther behind.

She progressed through the San Gabriel Mountains, with Los Angeles to the west and the Mojave Desert to the east. At the outskirts of the city smog, the air was crisp. Sweat evaporated almost as quickly as it formed.

She climbed nine-thousand-foot Mount Baldy, grateful to leave LA's exhaust and fumes behind. The PCT switchbacked sharply. Small rocks slithered from under her boots and rolled lazily down the mountainside. More than once she lost her footing and caught herself with her hiking poles.

A group of people approached from far below. Grace chose a smooth rock and sat to let them pass. Behind her lay the landscape she had crossed in the past days. She gazed across the miles.

I'll never get over covering all that on foot.

A solitary hiker interrupted her reverie. All she saw at first was a large brimmed sun hat on a tall, muscular body. Then, as he neared, she took in his regulation PCT beard and sunglasses.

Guys on the PCT look basically the same. Beards. Dark glasses. The only way to tell them apart is height and pack color. Except, of course, for the men in women's hiking skirts. Practicality over fashion. That kind of stands out.

Grace assessed the man's pack, shirt color, and size.

I don't think I've met him before.

She smiled.

He slowed his pace. "Taking a break?"

"Letting the group of you pass me."

"Oh, I'm not with them." He thrust a thumb down the hill. "That's the Sideways Seven down there."

"The party crowd? I've already heard a lot about them." Grace squinted down the trail. "I don't know how they do it. Partying and hiking. Those two words don't fit well into a sentence that has my name in it."

"Mine either. And they're always together. They never split up. I have to admit I don't get that." The man wiped thick, shaggy hair from his brow.

This guy's probably around my age. Nice bright eyes. They light up like fire. His face'd be attractive if it weren't so thin.

"I've been leapfrogging those guys most of the trail." He pulled his waist belt tighter. "I pass their camp in the morning. By noon they speed up and pass me. Sometimes there's a day or two between us, but we're sticking pretty close together, all things considered." He held out his hand. "I'm Beartrap, by the way."

Grace returned his strong grip. "Why Beartrap?"

"It's a mountain biking term for when you scrape your legs on the pedals. I was wearing shorts the first days out and my legs got pretty badly mangled in the bushes. Somebody gave me the name, and it stuck. I don't mind. I do some mountain biking, so it kind of fits. How about you?"

"Mountain biking? I used to when I was a kid, but I haven't in a long time."

"No." Beartrap chuckled. "I meant your name."

"Oh, sorry." Grace shook her head. "I'm Grace. Just Grace." The whisper of a smile crossed her lips.

"You have to be the only person I've met so far who doesn't have a trail name. Don't you like being anonymous?"

"I guess I don't. How are you ever supposed to find someone again once you're off the trail? People you want to keep in touch with could disappear forever."

Beartrap dusted his hands on his shorts. "I think maybe that's the point. Well, see you down the trail, Grace." He waved as he continued up the hill.

The Sideways Seven made rapid progress up the slope and were nearly on his heels. Grace studied their bodies as they soared by.

No outward sign of their dissipated lifestyle, that's for sure. Wiry and muscular, confident stride, upright stature. I'd pick them in a lineup as college athletes or Navy SEALs. They're talking and joking on the same incline that winded me. I thought I was fit. Guess not.

Beyond her, the group passed Beartrap.

How does he manage to keep up with them day after day?

That night, Grace befriended two older women camped near her tent. "Do you mind if I ask a stupid question? Why aren't hikers like the Sideways Seven leading the herd? They hike so fast."

The taller woman offered Grace a cookie. "Because they always lose a few days at resupply towns. They hit the bars, and that gives the other hikers a chance to catch up. You'll probably run into them again. They slow down whenever they take a few zeros."

"Zeros?"

"Days of hiking zero miles. Most thrus try to take as few zeros as possible. But people like the Sideways Seven dream about them."

"I doubt I'll ever catch up with them again at my slow pace. I'm becoming an expert at having people leave me behind. Passing other folks is a skill I'm working on."

The next morning, more hikers flew by her.

Am I still in the middle of the herd? Or am I falling back toward the tail end? And how the heck would I even know? When it starts getting awfully lonely out here? I don't want to pick up someone like Choir Master again. But it would be great to have someone to hike with. Especially if the main group is petering out soon.

At lunch, she sat at the top of a ridge with a group of fellow thrus. After eating, they packed up and Grace, once again, was left behind.

She consoled herself by reading Lone Star's latest note.

Just Grace,

What is it about you that brings out a side of me no one's ever seen before? Remember I told you I didn't like school? Well, thinking of you is making me think of things that would make Mrs. Pierson, my 10th grade English teacher, throw her hat over the windmill. Like this, from Tennyson, I think: So fold thyself, my dearest, thou, and slip into my bosom and be lost in me. See. I can do better than my own poem. Sweet dreams, my darling. Look up at the stars and think of me sharing that same blanket with you.

Lone Star

Thoughts of sharing a blanket and what they could do under the covers crowded upon her. She cocked her head.

Why is it suddenly so hot?

Grace jerked her mind back to the matter at hand.

Hiking in the herd's like driving on a busy freeway. There're always cars passing. But hiking alone at the back of the herd must be like driving on a country road at night. Secluded. Potentially scary.

She increased her pace.

That thought does it. The next person who catches up with me is going to be the one I hike with. I don't need to stay with them forever. But I could use a challenge.

Twenty minutes later, Grace heard the familiar sounds of someone approaching her from the rear. Instead of stepping to the side, she took a quick look back. The man walked at a steady lope, swinging long legs and arms. So she lengthened her stride.

Just my luck. A fast hiker.

She surged on. The dusty path circled the peak of Mount Hawkins. Grace puffed slightly in the thinner air. Conifers dotted the brown landscape with patches of dark green. Here and there small grey boulders clustered, the remains of avalanches.

No time to admire the view. He's gaining on me.

Minutes later she reconsidered.

This is silly. I'm too slow. If I want to hike with him, I should ask. Or would that make me look desperate? Like Choir Master.

After another branch in the trail, the PCT descended steeply to Windy Gap. The man picked up his pace. Grace panted.

Great. He's gaining on me. Like a rattle snake that's…whatever. No time for Texan metaphors. Only a few feet behind. I should be sensible. Let him pass.

She started down the slope and began an easy jog.

Let him think I do this all the time.

Her hiking poles fluttered behind her.

Real elegant, Grace. You probably look like a short Asian penguin.

A root tripped her. She flew into the air, twisted backwards, and landed on her pack. She slid down the mountain, bouncing off rocks and roots, spinning in circles. Her arms and legs flailed. For what felt like minutes, blue sky and branches sailed across her field of vision.

Then a man's voice said, "Gotcha."

Grace jerked to a halt. A huge pine tree obscured her view.

"That was close. You nearly collided with this tree." The man breathed heavily and leaned against the trunk. "Don't think that would have been pretty."

Grace thrashed her arms but couldn't turn over. The man hoisted her to her feet.

"You okay?"

Grace's face was smeared with dust. She brushed dust and needles from her legs and dropped her pack to the ground. "I'm fine." She couldn't bring herself to look the man in the eyes. "Thank you. That was totally idiotic of me."

The man stamped his feet and rubbed dirt from his hands. "Why were you running?"

Grace covered her face and mumbled through her fingers. "I wanted to keep up with you."

"You wanted to keep up with me?"

She lowered her hands. "Yes. I told myself I'd keep up with the next person who was going to pass me." His eyes met hers. "Not my brightest moment, huh?"

He scratched his beard. "Well, I guess everyone has to do something to pass the time out here. But if you want to hike together with someone, why don't you ask?"

"I'll remember to do that." Grace looked back. A long streak of brown dirt wound through the detritus of old twigs and branches littering the hill. "Wow. I fell all that way?"

"I had to cut across the switchback to get to you. Like I said, you were headed right for this tree." He patted the thick trunk.

"Another big mess. I was lucky. Again."

"You've done this before, then?"

"Not this. Other stupid things. I guarantee you I never slid down a mountain on my back before."

"First time for everything."

Grace took in her rescuer. Little was visible beyond the standard beard, sunglasses, and hat. He wore a dark t-shirt and shorts. His hands were large and solid. The muscles in his thin arms rippled when he moved.

They both stared at the skid marks. Grace felt suddenly faint.

"I feel a little weird asking." She inhaled deeply and let the air escape slowly between clenched teeth. "Do you mind if I give you a hug?"

"Not at all." The man laid his pack next to hers. White teeth gleamed and he held out his arms.

Grace lay her head against his chest. His shirt rubbed her cheek. A strong male scent of sweat and pheromones overwhelmed her senses. Arms encircled her torso and squeezed. Grace sighed.

Nice. But I wish it were Lone Star.

After a few seconds, she disengaged herself. "Thanks. I needed that. I don't think I've touched another person since Lake Morena. After one of my other close shaves."

"Also involving a rescue?"

"I'm lucky that way." She hoisted her pack.

"Well, happy to help. Any time." He gazed down the path ahead of them. "My name's Breeze. And, as it happens, I'm not in a particular hurry today. We can hike together for a bit if you want."

"Won't I slow you down?"

"I've already seen how fast you can go when you want to. I'm sure we can work something out."

CHAPTER 12

When in his late teens, Ed Galeano put one of his community college classmates into a day-long coma with a well-positioned punch to the bridge of his nose.

"You're lucky the bone didn't penetrate his brain." The dean turned his back to Ed and looked out the window at the concrete square that constituted the college's central green. "We're an inclusive community. We're sorry to see a student go. But we can't tolerate that type of behavior. We wish you the best."

Ed jerked his middle finger at the dean and then hastily adjusted the motion into a sweep of his hair as the man pivoted to look at him. Ed stood and left the room, slamming the door behind him.

He strode down the hallway muttering, punching bulletin boards, and kicking trash cans. "Who needs a fucking community college degree anyway? I'm better off finding a job." A campus police officer appeared. Ed spurted through the entrance doors, vaulted a hedge, and gave the officer the finger as he climbed a chain link fence.

Days after his expulsion, Ed trudged along Piedmont Avenue in Oakland, trailing a string of job application rejections behind him.

No work references. No family or friends. No college transcript. Of course nobody wants me, because I'm a total loser. Like my father.

He rushed past the maroon awnings of Fenton's Creamery, where he'd unsuccessfully applied for a job scooping ice cream. Next he sprinted to avoid the red-tiled Little Mao Mao Chinese, voted best of Oakland, where the owner had not even handed him an application. When a sign in the window of a one-story white stucco building proclaimed '*Help Wanted,*' Ed passed it quickly, head down. Then he returned for a second look.

The bicycle wheels hanging in the two arched windows intrigued him. He shoved open the glass entrance door and started when an old-fashioned bell tinkled as it shut behind him.

The store's fluorescent lighting failed to compete with the afternoon California sun. Ed's eyes took a minute to adjust. The air smelled of oil, hot rubber, and pine floor wax. Gradually, Ed made out a man at the cash register negotiating with a customer. He studied the clerk and assessed his best approach.

The older man was clean-shaven and wore outdated plastic glasses with large lenses that dropped to mid-cheek. His lined face was roasted a deep brown and contrasted starkly with the grey of his crew cut. He walked from behind the counter with a slight limp.

Might be ex-military. That could give me an

edge. He may be scared of robbery or mugging if he can't run. I'm a Navy brat who can act clean-cut. See how far that gets me.

When the customer left, Ed approached. "Excuse me, sir."

"Be right with you." The man glanced at Ed over his shoulder and disappeared through a back door.

Ed looked around the small store. Every available space was crammed with bicycles. There were rows standing on the floor and rows hanging from hooks in the ceiling.

"Sorry about the wait." The man placed a box of bicycle gloves near the register. "How can I help you?"

"I'm here about the sign in the window." Ed scanned the man's face for interest. "The help wanted sign? I'd most certainly appreciate the opportunity to apply, sir."

Dell Stoke raised an eyebrow. "You'd appreciate the opportunity, eh?"

"Yes, sir."

The man snorted. "Sir, is it? I haven't been called sir by a kid around here since my hair was brown." He ran fingers, black under the nails with grease, over his head. He regarded Ed with unveiled skepticism. "What kind of trouble you been in?"

"Trouble, sir? I'm not quite sure I know what you mean."

"I said, what kind of trouble you been in?"

Tiny beads of perspiration broke out on Ed's brow. He raised his hand to wipe them away, then caught himself and stood still.

"Don't lie to me now. That ain't no way to make

a first impression."

Ed's shoulders slumped. "Okay. My driver's license is suspended. I got arrested for DUI. Before that for petty theft. And last week they kicked me out of community college for punching some dude. I'll save you the trouble. You're not interested. I know." He turned toward the exit.

The old man chuckled and slapped his good leg. "Got most of it right. Figured on the DUI and the theft. Missed the college suspension."

"Expulsion. Sorry to have troubled you." Ed walked to the door.

"Whoa. Hold on there. Not so fast." Dell held out his hand like a school crossing guard. "You don't want to fill out an application form?"

"I thought…"

"You thought wrong. Come over to the register." Dell walked behind the counter, opened a cabinet, and took out a yellow legal pad. "What's your name?"

Ed told him and Dell scribbled it down without asking how it was spelled.

"Your address and phone? Got any work experience? What you know about bikes?"

He jotted down the answers. Ed chewed on his lower lip while Dell wrote a short paragraph and drew a line beneath it. He turned the block of paper to face Ed.

It read:

I, Edmundo Galeano, accept the part-time position of general gofer at Stoke's

Spokes. I will not steal, I will not come to work drunk, and I will be polite to customers. I will not fight with any of the other employees, no matter how obnoxious. I will be on time. I promise to do this, and Wendell Stoke promises to pay me two dollars above minimum wage.

When Ed finished reading, Dell pointed a stubby finger at a line at the bottom of the page. "Sign there and you got yourself a job."

Ed picked up the ballpoint pen and twisted it nervously in his fingers. He blinked and put it down. Then he looked from the paper to Dell and back again. Dell's square jaw shifted slowly, like a cow chewing cud.

"Take your time and think about it."

Ed picked up the pen, signed his name, hesitated, and added a medieval flourish under Galeano, feeling as though he were signing away his past.

A fresh start. A chance to make myself into something the world thinks I'm not.

***

Dell found plenty of things for the new hire to do around the shop. Ed dusted window exhibits, stocked display racks, cleaned wrenches, arranged bottles of lubricant, washed greasy rags, and chased after loose ball bearings by crawling around the shop floor with a magnet. Every task, large or small, took place under the watchful eye of Arnie, the head mechanic. Unlike Dell, Arnie recognized only the worst in Ed and treated him accordingly. Ed soon understood why Dell had made him promise not to fight with anyone.

"You blind? Missed that rag over there," Arnie would say, pointing to a reeking cloth he threw under a counter. Or, "Got a hot date tonight? Good luck looking like a desk jockey. You won't get that stain off your hands for a week. I put something special in the solvent." Ed looked at his dark blue hands and cursed under his breath. But the arrow hit home when Arnie attacked Ed's mother. "Bet she dumped you and ran. I can always tell. You got the look of a total loser. Your mom must've been counting the minutes 'til she could forget all about your sorry ass."

Dell observed the interactions between Arnie and Ed without comment. He stuck to the front of the store and let Arnie, the best bike mechanic in Oakland, run the back.

It's like Dell can read my mind, Ed thought. *I keep thinking, if Dell steps in, then I'm going to beat Arnie to a pulp. Don't care if I walk away in handcuffs. But he never steps in, and I end up thinking maybe it's not worth fighting over after all.*

Under Dell's watch, Ed walked away from every coarse comment, every push, every dirty rag thrown at his feet. He counted to fifty and stepped into the back alley to calm down.

***

Years later, watching Dell's coffin being lowered into the ground, Ed felt as though his past were being buried with it.

I'll make you proud, Dell.

As the new owner of Stoke's, he opened the shop early and stayed late. Early on a Saturday one May, he unpacked a box of helmets that had arrived the previous afternoon, stacking them on wire shelves next to the other accessories. The shop bell tinkled. Ed turned in surprise. An unscheduled customer before nine on a weekend was rare.

"Can I help you?"

A thin, long-haired youth in sagging jeans and an open-fronted Hawai'ian shirt stood before him. A broad, green and red snake tattoo slithered realistically across his midriff.

"Yeah, dude. I want to buy a Harley."

"'Fraid you're in the wrong store." Ed crossed his arms.

"Yeah, right." The guy tilted back his head and laughed. "Seriously, I wanna buy a bike."

Ed shoved the box of helmets under the rack. He spread his arms. "Looking for anything specific?"

"Uh huh." The man thrust his hands into his pockets. "A mountain bike. The best one you got in the store."

Ed smiled.

One of those customers. The ones who come in asking for a high-end item but leave with a basic Fuji or Trek. Fun to make this guy squirm.

"Certainly." Ed led him to the front of the shop. "The best we have is right over here." He pointed to a Cannondale Scalpel Ultimate in a position of honor. "That retails for just under ten grand."

Ed got the reaction he was looking for and almost whooped with laughter when he saw the man's eyes widen into saucers. "Perhaps you'd like to custom order? People who want the highest quality usually order the frame separately. Then they hang on the best parts they can afford. I could easily help you build something."

The guy looked around at the bike skeletons Ed pointed out. No tires. No pedals. No gears. He shuffled his feet. "Lemme talk to the owner."

"You're looking at him." Ed enunciated each syllable.

The youth's face brightened. "So what do you ride, dude? You're the owner. You must have something fancy."

"What I ride is right over here." Ed indicated a shiny bicycle with everything attached.

The guy looked at him. "You didn't make your bike out of parts? I thought that was the best."

Ed reddened. "This is an excellent bike. I'm a busy guy. Got a store to run, you know?"

The young man lifted the price tag and looked. He nodded. "Is this my size?"

Ed assessed him, from his torn purple tennis shoes to his long, scruffy hair. "You're about my height. So that's the correct size."

"Okay, I'll take it." The young man's hands fiddled in his pockets. "Does it come in any other colors?"

Ed stared. "No, this is it."

"Fine." The guy scratched his head and looked around the store. "What else do I need? A helmet?

Gloves?"

"Yes." A shade of respect tinged Ed's voice. "You'll need those."

"Awesome." The guy's eyes twinkled. "What you got for a helmet?"

Ed outfitted him with an exact replica of his own favorite biking gear. Helmet, gloves, shorts, jersey, shoes, socks, a hydration pack, and sunglasses accumulated in a pile on the counter.

Ed rang up the total. "How're you paying?"

"Cash, dude." The man brought his hands out of his pockets. Each fist clutched a roll of bills.

Ed raised an eyebrow. "The total's over five thousand dollars."

"It's all good. I robbed a bank."

Ed raised both eyebrows.

"I'm messing with you, man. I totaled my car and cashed the insurance check yesterday. Thought I'd better get a safer set of wheels, you know? Since I got no license."

Ed chuckled. "I have some experience with that myself." He handed the man the receipt. "Hold on to that and don't take the tags off, in case something doesn't fit. But you should be good."

The guy raised his chin in a quick nod. "Thanks. I'm Jerry Kriebel, by the way. Glad to do business with you." He rolled the bike out of the store. "People'll think we're twins." He waved over his shoulder as he pushed his new purchase down the street.

***

The next day Ed asked Officer Turangeo to wait while he closed the shop. He told the wide-eyed mechanics to go home early and pulled two swivel stools together in the back.

Arnie didn't leave, straightening tools and folding rags.

"Arnie, get out of here. Now."

Arnie picked up an insulated lunch bag. He shuffled out the back door and closed it carefully behind him.

"Have a seat." Ed rolled a stool toward the officer. "And before you get started, I'm not under arrest or anything, right?"

"I have some questions for you, Mr. Galeano, about the accident on Mount Tamalpais with that little girl. Where were you at around eight yesterday morning?"

"Yesterday? I was out mountain biking."

"And where was that, exactly?" The officer removed a small paper pad and pen from his jacket pocket.

Ed's throat dried up. He coughed to clear it. "Around Mount Tam."

The officer's eye twitched. "Can you be more specific?"

Ed rose and retrieved a bike trail map from the front of the store. He spread it on the workshop counter, took a pen, and traced a route. "I parked here, at the lot across from the Mountain Home Inn."

"Uh huh." Officer Turangeo jotted notes. "About what time did you get to the parking lot?"

"Around seven thirty, I guess."

"Okay. What did you do next?"

"I rode up here." Ed pointed to a trail to the north. "Then around here, and here, and then down there and, after this, back to the car." He traced a long loop on the map. The winding path crossed Mount Tam, circled two lakes, snaked down to Stinson Beach, and climbed the mountain west of Muir Woods. "It's about thirty-five miles."

"How long did that take you?"

"About six hours. I stopped for a bit at Stinson Beach." Ed poked the map.

"Did anyone see you on this ride?"

"Yes." He looked the officer in the eyes. "Someone saw me. Actually, it's kind of funny. See, I met this woman in the parking lot."

"In the parking lot across from the Mountain Home Inn?"

"Yeah. She parked near me and had trouble getting her bike off one of those trunk racks, you know? They're kind of tricky. I helped her. We got talking. She was wearing one of those lycra body suits, the kind where you can see everything although you can't see anything..." The officer drummed his fingers on the counter. "Anyway, I invited her to join me."

"Then what happened?"

"We did what I said. We followed this route." He pushed the map closer to the officer. "I split my lunch with her when we got to the beach. We ended up back at the parking lot." Ed's voice petered out.

"And then?"

"Well, she came back to my place."

"In your car?"

"No, she followed me in hers."

"Did she spend the night?"

"No. She left around nine."

"So you're saying you have an alibi from seven thirty in the morning until nine at night? I'm sure you won't mind if we check that out with her?"

"Uh, no. I guess not."

"I hope not. What's her name?" Officer Turangeo poised pen over pad.

"Well, that's the thing." Ed ran his hands through his hair. "I didn't actually get her name."

"You mean her full name. What's her first name?"

"I don't know."

The officer's pen tapped the counter. "You expect me to believe you spent the whole day with this woman and never got her name?"

"It wasn't that kind of a day. We were mostly riding bikes. You don't talk when you're riding."

"And during the evening activities?"

"It never came up."

"So can you describe anything about her? Her car? Her license plate number? Anything that would help identify her?"

"She had short red hair. Kind of straight…" His eyes roamed the ceiling as he searched his brain for information. "Her nose was…well, kind of normal, I guess. In general, she had this…normal kind of face. Pretty. With freckles, I think. One thing was unusual. She had this insane set of piercings around her…" He drew circles on his chest. "You know."

"Her nipples."

"Yeah. There were these rods and studs that

made a heart." Ed held up his thumbs and forefingers to demonstrate. "There can't be many people who have something like that."

"Probably not. But it's not exactly a feature we can post on a milk carton. Besides red hair, what else can you remember?"

"Her car was blue, I think. Or maybe brown? Anyway, it was a sedan. I think a Japanese model. I wasn't paying attention." He closed his eyes. "She had one of those air freshener things dangling over the dash."

Officer Turangeo stared at him.

The counter squeaked as Ed leaned on it. "I know I sound like an idiot. But you have to believe me. I didn't know I was going to have to describe this to anyone."

"The car's probably going to help us the most right now." Officer Turangeo snapped the notepad shut.

"So, I'm in the clear, right?"

The officer stood. "I wouldn't say that. We have to find this woman to confirm your alibi. Right now the evidence against you is only circumstantial. Still." He paused and stood in the doorway that led back to the store. "Don't leave town without letting us know."

Ed exhaled as though he'd been punched.

I can't believe this. Getting laid was all I was thinking about yesterday.

Ed blurted one final thought at the door to the street. "You said someone identified me. That's not possible."

"A resident near the scene said he waved to you.

You rode your bike past his car about ten minutes before the accident."

"I don't remember seeing anyone. Who was it?"

"I'd rather not say at the moment." The officer opened the door. "I'll be in touch. If you have any questions or remember anything else, call the Mill Valley Police Department. Have a nice day."

Ed locked the door. Out of the corner of his eye he glimpsed Arnie exiting the alley that led to the back of the store.

The glass door rattled as he unlocked it and flung it open. "You fucking bastard. You spying scum."

Arnie stopped and smirked. "I don't know what you're talking about. But if the back door was cracked and I heard you making up shit, well, it's public property."

"Don't you dare spread lies about me in the shop. I have an alibi." He marched up to Arnie and shoved him.

"Whoa, man." Arnie brushed his polo shirt with exaggerated care. "You better think about what you're doing before you start anything. You got enough trouble coming your way."

Ed held up his fist. "They're going to find her."

"What? That dream woman you said you laid?"

"She was real."

"What's gonna be real is those guys who go after your pretty ass in prison, man." Arnie sneered.

Ed sucked in a deep breath. He lowered his hand. "You're fired, Arnie. Get out of here before I do something you'll regret."

Arnie stared but didn't move. "I worked here before you were born, punk." His mouth curled into a snarl and his tone dropped. "You do this, and you're going down. I'll bring you down, man."

"I'm not scared of you."

Arnie looked him in the eyes. "You should be scared. Real scared."

***

Over the course of the following week, customer traffic dropped off sharply. By Friday evening it was clear something unusual had happened. Posts about Ed flooded Yelp, Google, and biking blogs. Vitriolic, insinuating comments hinted at his involvement in the now famous hit-and-run that put a little girl into a coma. He read veiled accusations staying slightly to the right of slander that emphasized his police record, past threats of violence, and lack of a concrete alibi. Many posts referenced the confrontation with his head mechanic.

Ed lay sleepless that night, his mind unable to stop swirling from the injustice of his situation. Toward morning, he only half noticed an off-hours documentary about an annual gathering of twins in Ohio. In the middle of scenes from the Double Take Parade, Ed jerked awake.

Twins. That's the answer. "People will think we're twins." The guy who bought all the bike gear the day before the accident. Jerry something. He had my bike. My clothes. He must have been the one. Why didn't I think of him sooner?

Ed swung out of bed, feeling lighter.

This will give the police something to investigate.

136

He left Officer Turangeo a voice mail and got a call back in the late morning.

Exasperation flowed through the connection. "You don't have a credit card receipt. You have a shoddy description of the man. Most importantly, once again, you don't have a name. Do you know how many Jerry's there are in greater San Francisco? Hell, I'll even narrow it down to Oakland for you. Jerry's short for Jerome, Gerald, and Jeremy, for starters."

Ed turned the phone, talking directly to the screen, as if being face to face with the officer's voice could help convince him. "But I don't have a bar code reader in the store. We only have handwritten receipts. They're not specific. And the guy paid in cash."

"If you remember more, give me another call."

"I'm not lying."

"Right." Officer Turangeo sighed. "Look, Mr. Galeano, we can't arrest you, because we've got nothing concrete, but we'll be watching…and waiting. I'd keep my hands clean and stay well under the radar if I were you."

"I'll remember his name."

"Good luck with that." Officer Turangeo hung up.

In the evening, Ed analyzed the public Facebook pages of Oakland's Jeremys, Geralds, Jarreds, and Jeromes, looking for a clue. He sent friend requests until Facebook blocked him for phishing.

Maybe the guy doesn't have a nickname. Maybe Jerry is Jerry.

That's how he found him: Jerry Kriebel. A guy

with a green and red snake tattoo crawling across his profile photo.

The next morning, he shared his news with Officer Turangeo.

"How do I know you didn't pick some person off Facebook at random?"

Ed almost threw the phone across the room in frustration. He sucked in a quick breath. "I told you yesterday his name was Jerry and said he had a tattoo. Now I found Jerry with a tattoo. The *same* tattoo. Can't you see it all fits?"

"We'll look into it. But don't start thinking you can accuse anyone you like of a crime."

"Are you kidding? What about me? Aren't I being accused?" Ed's hand trembled. "If you don't look into this, I'm going to find Jerry myself and bring him to you. I don't care how long it takes."

"Watch your step, Mr. Galeano." His voice had the ominous rumble of thunder on a clear blue day. "That girl's getting better, but she's not going to walk again. Don't involve any more innocent victims."

"Innocent? Jerry Kriebel's not innocent. He's the one who did it." Ed punched the *end call* button and hurled the phone onto the sofa.

Most of Jerry's information on Facebook was private, but his page displayed his likes. Photos abounded of a large selection of scrubby East Bay punk bands.

I'll conduct my own goddamned investigation.

But months and innumerable punk band concerts later, he knew nothing more about Jerry. And business at Stoke's had sunk to an all time low.

Previous five-star ratings had plummeted to two. Competition in the surrounding area drew away existing customers who had second thoughts.

The foreclosure sale happened on a sunny afternoon in late March.

The same day, Ed sold his furniture and moved into a room in a San Leandro Bay motel, a noisy location between US 880 and razor wire protected warehouses. It was the kind of motel where pickups and old sedans crawled into the parking lot after midnight in the semi-darkness of one working floodlight and couples of all descriptions disembarked, eager to find a room for a few hours of passion, lust, or employment. Night after night, he stared out his window at the continual human parade. More than once in the following weeks he startled awake in the early morning, roused by the rhythmic knocking of his neighbor's headboard.

As the time between his old and new lives grew, his finances shrunk. He grew a beard to save on shaving supplies. When his contact lens supply ran out, he reverted to squinting and guessing at street signs. He bummed laundry detergent off hookers at the laundromat.

Pale, haggard, and gaunt, he knew few of his friends would have recognized him. The only reminders of his previous existence were his computer and his bicycle. The room's rattling window air conditioner propped up his Gary Fisher Superfly, with its dusty handlebars leaning forlornly against drawn curtains. He spent most waking hours using the motel's spotty Wi-Fi to search for signs of Jerry.

I'm not leaving Oakland until I've settled the score.

One evening at the Stork Club, a raucous dive on Telegraph Avenue, Ed began a conversation he'd had a hundred times previously.

He cornered a blue-haired youth in black leather and chains at the bar. "Ever heard of Jerry Kriebel?"

"Jerry Kriebel? Sure, I know him." The youth's voice floated through the thump of the music. "Used to share a house with a buddy of mine. What's it to you?"

Ed clutched the counter. "You know him? You're sure?"

"Guy with a snake tattoo on his chest, right?" His blue hair caught the strobe lights as he threw back half a beer.

Ed held his breath. "That's him."

"Yeah. Well, that's the Jerry I'm talking about. Like I said. What's it to you?" He swayed unsteadily, his eyes trying to focus on Ed but frequently missing, fixing instead on the crowd or the floor.

Ed took him by both arms and shook him gently. "The police want to ask him a few questions."

The guy jerked away. "Shit, man. You a cop?"

Ed raised both hands and shook his head violently. "No. I'm interested in finding him before they do."

"Oh." The youth winked, moved closer, and reduced the amplitude of his voice. "That's broken of you, dude. But, you know, last I heard, Jerry's safe. He's in LA. That's, like, almost across state lines."

"LA?" The pounding din hid the surprise in Ed's voice.

"Yeah. I hear there's some slamming rager that starts around Mexico and lasts all summer. The only fucked up part is you gotta walk millions of miles. But Jerry says he's gonna do it."

Ed leaned in until the two were almost touching noses. "What? A party? In Mexico?"

Hot breath blew against Ed's face. "Not *in* Mexico. At the border. It's on some hiking trail called the PCP or LSD or something. Supposed to be a tight blowout. But you gotta hike. Carry a backpack. Now, me? I don't want to carry anything heavier than a beer." He bent over the bar. "Gimme another."

Ed grabbed the guy's shoulder and spun him back around. "You're sure? You're sure Jerry's doing this hike? Do you know when he's starting?"

"Safe, man." The youth flipped his blue hair aside and tossed down his new drink. "Buddy of mine got a text from him yesterday. Told me all about it, 'cause he couldn't fucking believe it. He's starting next weekend."

Ed pumped the man's free hand.

"Hey, no need to thank me. Like I said. LA's practically Nevada. Don't think the law'll find him there."

Ed pushed his way to the exit. Rain soaked him to the skin as he leaned, breathless, against the iron grills of the dollar store next door. His head spun as he rattled the bars, shouting profanities intended for Jerry. Passersby hardly glanced at him. On Telegraph Avenue at one in the morning, he

141

blended into the crowd.

Later that night, he searched the Internet and found the trail.

The Pacific Crest Trail. PCT. Jerry's there. I'm going.

The next day, he sold his bike and laptop. An Army-Navy surplus store supplied him with a large backpack that he filled with things he thought he would need: boots, a cold weather sleeping bag, water bottles, and a ten-pound tent the guy in the store called "ultralight."

Three days after the visit to the Stork Club, Ed boarded the CA Shuttle Bus bound for Los Angeles.

He sat near the front and gazed absently at the boarding passengers. A hunched, white-haired man held onto the backrest of each seat as he swayed toward empty spots at the rear.

Looks like Dell.

Ed brushed the thought from his mind like an annoying fly. The bus jerked away from the station. He patted the pocket of his jacket and caressed the reassuring bulk of his new Navy pilot survival knife with its five-inch blade.

Who cares what he would think of me now.

CHAPTER 13

Breeze and Grace hiked together after her unplanned slide down the mountain. But after a few hours, he sped on ahead.

"Short legs. Who knew they'd make me so antisocial?" She watched his figure retreat into the growing dusk.

She ran across him again two days later at the top of a ridge. He sat on a rock, boots removed, staring anxiously at his toes. When he saw Grace, he limped toward her. They greeted with a warm embrace.

"Funny meeting you again so soon." Breeze squeezed her shoulder.

"Yeah. At the rate you were going, I thought you'd be at Hiker Heaven by now."

"I did too. But I've been having some trouble with my toes." He lifted a foot and wiggled five digits. "They don't seem to like my boots anymore. So I'm slowing down. I think I'm going to need to get new footwear in Agua Dulce."

"Maybe your toe problem will even out our

speeds. Hiker Heaven's still about sixty miles. Do you want some company?"

Breeze glanced at her and then shot a look down the trail. He shook his head. "No. I'm going to do it real slow. I don't want to permanently mess up my feet. You keep going, Grace. I'll catch up with you again one of these days, once I get myself a new pair of shoes." He hobbled back to his rock.

A gust blew tiny sand eddies across the path. The wind died and the dust settled.

Go with the flow.

"Take care of your feet." She shrugged her pack higher on her shoulders. "I'm going to spend a few days at Hiker Heaven, so maybe we'll overlap there. If not, catch up with me later, okay?"

"Will do. For sure."

Later, at Hiker Heaven, Grace leafed through the register. The hiker paradise comprised a collection of RVs and tents set up with deluxe cots, washing machines, loaner clothes, a kitchen, a barbecue, a TV, Internet access, and showers. Almost all PCT thru-hikers stopped there.

Except Lone Star, wouldn't you know it? How could he have skipped this place?

Grace closed the register and sighed.

Not even his signature. And nobody's heard about him recently.

A chill of loneliness crept from the pit of her stomach through her limbs.

Stop it. The man who wrote that last stanza isn't going to forget me.

The water brought you strength to try.

144

Your smile shone bright and true.
The pulsing joy I shared with you
Still lifts me to the sky.

She asked around for Breeze. No one had seen him either.

That night, Grace shared a tent with ten other thrus.

Why are trail guys always rescuing me from disaster? Men never rushed out of nowhere in San Francisco. Like that time I almost stepped in front of a bus. Plenty of guys on the sidewalk. Nobody grabbed me. All I got was hearing loss from the stupid bus horn.

I sure hope there aren't too many law firms in El Paso. I might have to call them all and ask if they have a thru-hiking attorney on staff. One who knows poetry.

She fished out her phone and read another note.

...Now slides the silent meteor on, and leaves a shining furrow, as thy thoughts in me.

Her lips pursed. Something in the nether regions of her torso pulsed a rhythmic beat. She pulled the sleeping bag down to her waist and cradled the phone.

Now slides the silent meteor on...

With Lone Star filling her mind and an uncharacteristically soft cushion for her back, Grace tossed and turned until an hour later, she finally drifted to sleep.

She stayed two nights at Hiker Heaven, calling Celine to discuss plans and future drop boxes, rearranging gear, buying supplies. But the camp had a two-night limit.

I can't waste time waiting for something that might never happen. Maybe Lone Star's up ahead waiting for me after all.

She awoke her final morning to the smell of coffee. She blinked.

Fresh brewed? Out here?

She dressed and followed the scent. It led to a propane camp stove like the one she'd carried before her Idyllwild makeover. A two-person tent perched on the lawn behind it. A short, slender man with round tortoiseshell glasses and a bald spot evident through thinning brown hair crouched next to the flame. He looked up.

"My nose had to see if it was right." Grace's expression softened into a smile of reminiscence. "I haven't smelled fresh coffee since Lake Morena."

"Have a seat." The man indicated the lawn. "I'll give you a cup." He turned to an approaching thick-set woman with a microfiber towel slung around her neck. "Folger, can this woman borrow your pot?"

"By all means."

Folger seated herself next to Grace on the grass. Hefty thighs stretched her light green hiking shorts as she crossed her legs.

"The smell usually brings someone over to our tent most mornings." Straight grey hair pulled back in a short ponytail emphasized Folger's oval face. Boiling water coursed over coffee grounds in a small golden filter. "We've got to have fresh brewed, right, Max?" She handed Grace the pot. "Milk?"

"You've got milk too?"

"Only today." The fine lines around Folger's eyes crinkled with a secret smile. "We're leaving this morning. We got a small carton at the grocery store yesterday for a treat. Tell me when."

Grace let her pour enough to turn the coffee a creamy brown and took a sip.

"Wow." She held the pot away from her and admired it. "This is fantastic. I forgot what it tasted like. I used to drink four cups a day." She took another sip. "I went cold turkey before starting this hike."

"Most people do. That's how we got our trail names. Max is short for Maxwell House."

"Do you want to stay for breakfast?" Max offered Grace a peach. "We did too much shopping yesterday. We'll never be able to eat it all without help."

The early morning sun warmed Grace's back as peach juice dribbled onto her hands and legs. After six peaches, Max served her a pot of oatmeal with blueberries and raisins. Then she ate two bananas and a chocolate muffin.

"I didn't think I'd be much help in reducing your supply. But I guess I was wrong." Grace patted her distended stomach. "I'll never get over how much I eat out here." She lay back and looked at the silky white clouds streaking the sky. "A full belly at the start of another day of hiking. My idea of heaven."

Folger and Grace carried the assortment of pots

and utensils to the communal sink. Folger scrubbed her pot with a Brillo pad. Errant suds flew to her nose, and she wiped it with the back of her hand. "You're leaving this morning too?"

"Yes." Grace concentrated on the coffee filter. "I was waiting for someone. This guy, actually. Lone Star. I hiked with him for a bit. I hoped he might show up here. But I'm beginning to see that's silly. Always wanting things to be different."

"Ah, so that's how it is."

"I know we'll get back together. He's the one for me and I'm not letting go. I just have to learn to be more patient."

Grace left camp at ten, struggling with a pack heavy with new supplies. She followed Agua Dulce Canyon Road through town. At the junction where the PCT began a slow ascent into the surrounding hills, she noticed two figures on the trail ahead of her and was close upon them before she realized who they were. Folger and Max parted to let her pass.

"Thought you might catch up with us if we took it easy." Max's glasses sparkled in the bright light. "We're always glad of a little company on the trail."

Grace looked at Folger.

Did she tell him I'm lonely?

But when the PCT branched off from the dirt road and became a narrow path again, Max encouraged Grace to go first. "We don't want to hold you up."

"Thanks. Maybe you'll catch up later."

She strode up the gentle ascent, swinging her hiking poles in time to "The Happy Wanderer," always buzzing in her brain since her Choir Master encounter. In the next hour, every time she looked over her shoulder at the bizarre rocky vistas and the mountains she'd passed days earlier, there were Max and Folger, not far behind. She waved to them. They waved back.

She took a lunch break on the ridge between Spunky and Bouquet Canyons and reassessed her plans.

They hike at my speed, but I avoid them because I'm trying to be happy alone. How stupid is that?

When Max and Folger approached her lunch spot, Grace waited until they unpacked their sandwiches.

"Would you mind if we hiked together for a bit? I'd enjoy the company."

Folger and Max exchanged a glance. "We'd love it." Folger sipped from a water bottle. "We find hiking in a group to be quite pleasant, don't we, Max?"

Max nodded and finished his mouthful. "I admire people who hike alone, but Folger and I have always done it together. There's a lot to be said for having someone else to talk to now and again."

"Still, if you meet someone else or want to slow down or speed up, that's fine." Folger patted Grace's knee. "We won't feel insulted. And don't feel obligated to keep us company if there are younger folks around. You've probably heard it already, but there's an expression on the trail. Hike your own hike. We think it's a good rule to live by, don't we, dear?"

Max's mouth was full again. But he squeezed his wife's hand.

***

That same evening, in the town of Saugus, south of Hiker Heaven, Ed Galeano slinked into the Rattlers Bar-B-Que restaurant. His eyes squinted in the dim light as he scanned the room.

The Sideways Seven sat in a row at the bar. Salsa, chips, and beer lined the counter in front of them. Ed looked at his watch.

Happy Hour. They'll stay till it's over.

Ed chose a dark table in a corner from where he could watch the group's raucous antics.

Perfect. Jerry just pinched the tip from that table. Things are looking up. Maybe they'll get kicked out again.

Ed's teeth tore into a sticky rib. He sucked sauce from his fingers.

Scum. You deserve everything that's coming to you.

CHAPTER 14

"What brought you to the PCT?" Max sat next to Grace their first evening together while Folger stirred a large pot over their stove. "I know you said your brother wanted to do this. But that can't be the whole story."

"The short answer of how I got here is Celine."

"She's a thru?"

Grace inspected her feet for hot spots. "She was Kenji's girlfriend, so the girlfriend of a wannabe thru."

Max handed her a bottle of blister powder. "That's almost as good."

Folger looked up. "Better."

Grace sprinkled the powder in her socks. "I had all his gear, food, everything. Things piled all over my condo's floor. I thought I was ready. But Celine kept saying I had to read those PCT books. Or join the listserv. Or get the PCT app."

"Did you listen?" Folger dished lumpy stew into camp bowls.

"I was too busy concentrating on food prep. She

pointed out I wouldn't need food if I didn't go. But I told her I was kind of having fun testing things out. Like one week of only Rice-A-Roni. Did you know there are over fifteen different flavors, and that's not including Pasta Roni?"

"I've got three kinds right here." Max nudged his white pack with his foot.

"I decided on one I liked on Monday, but by Thursday I never wanted to eat it again."

"It's different at home than when you're out on the trail."

"Tell me about it. Even crappy food tastes awesome when you've hiked twenty miles. I've been known to tear packages apart and lick the insides."

Folger handed Grace an empty foil packet. "You can have the rest of my tuna."

Grace studied the package. "Okay. I'm not proud." She ripped the sides. Oil smeared her chin as she smacked her lips.

"So did you ever read the books?" Folger blew on her steaming bowl.

"No. Celine came over at Christmas and I finally told her what was holding me back. I knew it sounded crazy but the hike seemed like the answer to all the questions I had. My sister was moving to Atlanta and my parents had put their house up for sale. I didn't want to be left behind. I felt like the hike would get me going."

Folger lifted her eyebrows.

"I know. It was only slightly this side of insane."

Folger cocked her head to one side. "You think?"

"Maybe totally insane. But I didn't read any of

the books or look at the websites because I was afraid the risks would freak me out."

"Wouldn't being prepared make it less risky?"

"Sure. But once I learned about everything that could go wrong, I'd start imagining all kinds of disasters, decide it was too dangerous, and not go. I'd be right back where I started. Everyone else moving on and me…well, with me being me."

"Did Celine understand?"

"She agreed to be my base camp. She said that I was going to kick the PCT's ass. Then she said the desert was serious shit. I almost choked."

Folger and Max flashed her questioning looks.

Grace smirked. "Because I thought the trail was only in the mountains. So Celine took me to REI that same night. Said they'd know what I should do. And in the car she asked me to remind her to ask the clerks about crampons."

"Wait." Folger inspected Grace's face. "Don't tell me. You didn't know what crampons were."

"I knew what they were." Grace paused, then grinned. "But I didn't know there would be snow on the PCT. I'd just gotten used to the desert idea."

"I'm amazed you're here." Max swished out his empty bowl with a few drops of water.

"So am I, sometimes. Teva, this thru I met a while ago, promised that there'd be some moment when I knew I was a thru. So I've been waiting for a single instant. But I think instead, this whole hike's changed me. I don't think about home anymore. I'm used to life on the trail. And the best part of the PCT is the one I'm walking along. I guess all that makes me a thru."

Folger disengaged the stove from the small can of gas and packed both items in a stuff sack. "That. And licking out the tuna fish package."

CHAPTER 15

Together, Grace, Max, and Folger traversed Jeep roads, dusty trails, and miles of the Los Angeles Aqueduct. The PCT in this section meandered through mostly low, monotonous lands where parched brown earth sprouted green creosote shrubs and infrequent, freakish Joshua trees. The sun beat down mercilessly and water was scarce again.

After seven days of hiking, they reached Highway 58. The resupply towns were Tehachapi to the west and Mojave to the east. Celine's drop box waited at the post office in Mojave. But Folger and Max were going to Tehachapi.

"We'll see you again soon, Grace." Max kissed her cheek. "On or off the trail."

"I'll find you." Grace kissed his rough whiskers and gave Folger a long hug. "I've got your real names. And you've got mine."

In Mojave, Grace checked into a hotel and spent an hour in the shower, scrubbing. Dark ridges of dust and grime circled her ankles. Lines of sweat and dirt demarcated the edges of her shirt. Mud rimmed her fingernails.

I need a Brillo pad. The trail doesn't like to let go.

She washed her clothes in the sink and lay on the bed in the air conditioning until her hiking skirt and t-shirt were dry.

Her feet, light without her pack, flew the few blocks to the post office. Torn envelopes and empty stamp booklets littered the main room's table. Grace flipped through the worn spiral bound hiker register. Names she recognized filled the pages. But there was no hint of Lone Star.

Max and Folger would have called if his name had been in the Tehachapi register.

Grace trudged with slumped shoulders to Mike's Roadhouse Café, where the menu in the window lifted her spirits slightly.

With all this walking, I lose weight no matter how much I eat. But it sure is fun trying not to.

She chose a rear-facing booth and perused the possible selections. The teenage waitress didn't blink when Grace ordered a bowl of homemade chili, a burrito with extra cheese, rice and beans, a side of coleslaw, a side of fries, and an extra thick malted vanilla milkshake.

"You want it all at the same time?" The young woman cracked her gum and shoved the order pad into the breast pocket of her freshly ironed blouse.

"Bring it as you make it."

Halfway through her burrito, Grace jumped at a tap on her shoulder. She looked up with a mouth full of cheese and beef.

"Beartrap." The man pointed to himself.

"Remember? We met on Mount Baldy. You're the no-trail-name woman. Grace, right?" He stuck out his hand. "Nice to see you again."

"That's right." Grace sputtered lettuce and rice and motioned for him to take the seat across from her. He remained standing and let her finish chewing. "It's good to see you too. I didn't recognize you at first without your pack. Beartrap was something to do with bike pedals, wasn't it?"

"That's right."

The restaurant door opened and a group of twenty-somethings sauntered in.

"I haven't dug in yet." Her hand again indicated the spot in her booth. "You're welcome to join me."

Beartrap cast his eyes toward the people entering and shook his head. "No, thanks. I've got some shopping to do. Just wanted to say hello. Happy trails." He held up his hand in a farewell and was out the door before Grace could respond.

She shrugged and returned to her meal. Out of the corner of her eye she glimpsed seven men and women with farmer tans and loose shorts sitting near the entrance.

Must be thrus.

She bit into her burrito.

Maybe those Sideways Seven I saw before.

Grace meandered back to her hotel in the cool evening breeze. A plastic bag with two slices of cherry pie swung at her side. Celine's resupply box was tucked under her other arm. A small paper bag perched on top of the box, filled with fresh fruit from the supermarket she'd noticed on the way.

Her second floor room overlooked the pool. She

fished the plastic key card out of her shorts while children in pastel suits splashed each other in the shallows. Short-sleeved adults clustered under striped umbrellas and watched, surrounded by plastic soda bottles. A tall man with dripping hair and shorts that hung precariously on jutting hip bones waved in her direction.

Another thru?

She held up her bags and wiggled them. He gestured he was coming up. She entered her room and left the door ajar.

A minute later, a knock announced Breeze. He stepped in, toweling his hair. "Hey, Grace. I thought it was you." He sat down on the king-size bed and leaned back on his hands.

"Breeze." Grace's' face registered intermingled surprise and pleasure. "What are you doing here?"

"Same thing as you, I imagine."

"Resupply?"

"Yep."

"Well, you're a sight for sore eyes." Grace pulled the desk chair toward the bed and sat. "I've been hiking with an older couple and got used to having people around. I wasn't looking forward to spending an evening by myself."

"It's nice to see you too." Breeze ran his thickly lashed brown eyes appreciatively over Grace's thin frame. "I got in yesterday. Took a zero today." He reclined farther on his elbows and crossed his legs with one ankle resting on his knee. The bed quivered.

Grace flushed. She hopped lightly from her chair and busied herself arranging the peaches in a straight line on the small desk.

"I'm here for a one-nighter too. I mean, a one-night stay. That is…I'm heading out first thing tomorrow."

Breeze lay completely back and let his arms flop open. "Too bad." His legs swung rhythmically, bumping the side of the bed, making the air vibrate. "We could have some fun together here."

Grace caught her breath.

Breeze's legs stopped swinging. He sat up and locked eyes with her. She turned away.

Nice try, Breeze. But you lack a certain Texas something.

"Want some pie?" She held up the plastic container. "We could eat it by the pool."

Breeze shrugged and looked toward the door. "I never say no to pie. I'll meet you down there."

After he left, Grace exhaled slowly.

Wow. Guess I'm not the only one who's spent months without sex.

She fished in her pack for a tank top and quick-drying shorts. Down by the pool, children screeched and cannonballed. Grace jumped in and splashed water at the kids from the sides. Breeze swam erratic laps. Later, at a plastic table, they shared the pie and talked about hiking, gear, and the weather.

She was licking gooey red ooze from her fingers when a woman's terrified scream interrupted her.

"My son's drowning. Wade!"

A large brunette in a purple sarong bounced poolside.

Breeze's chair clattered to the ground as he dashed to the edge and scanned the depths. Before

Grace understood what was happening, Breeze dove in. Grace approached the screaming mother, transfixed by the scene unfolding in the pool. Below the shimmering blue surface, the deep end drain gripped the boy's hand. Breeze worked to free him. Legs kicked. Arms struggled.

After interminable seconds, two figures rose to the surface. Breeze hoisted the boy under his armpits. Grace pulled him onto the concrete. The boy coughed and spluttered. She turned his head sideways and he retched yellow water onto his mother's silver manicured toes. A crowd formed around them and clapped.

"Wade…" The mother sobbed and stroked the boy's wet hair.

Breeze pulled himself out of the water and leaned over the child. "You okay?"

"I won't ever let him in the water again." His mother buried the boy's brown hair in a fluffy American flag towel. She turned to Breeze. "What you did. It was a miracle. You dove right in. I just stood there." She reached for Breeze's hand and kissed it.

Breeze rolled his eyes, but not before Grace noticed a sparkle of pleasure. "It was nothing, Anybody would have done the same thing."

"Wade, honey, you come with Mommy. Let's get you into bed. You've had a big scare." She bundled the boy in her towel and led him toward the first floor rooms.

"Okay." Grace slapped Breeze playfully on the arm. "For the record, you *were* amazing. I've seen you save someone from near death twice now. First me. Now Wade."

A pleased look passed over Breeze's face before he could suppress it.

"You're quite a man." Grace shook his hand. "We should get some reporters out here to take down your story."

Breeze shot a glance at the street and suddenly yanked Grace toward him, clasping her body tightly against his. His lips pressed against hers in a kiss filled with demand and desire. Hands ran through her wet hair as he bent over her.

Blood rushed in her ears. Then she pushed her hands gently against his shoulders.

He pulled her body upward, lifting her onto her tiptoes. She pushed away harder.

"No." She freed herself from his embrace. "I'm sorry. But no."

A flash of light blinded her. Headlamp beams careened across their bodies in the growing twilight. Whistles and catcalls pierced the remaining poolside chatter.

"Who's that?" Grace held up her arm to protect her eyes.

The look on Breeze's face indicated he had to remind himself of his surroundings. "I think it's the Sideways Seven. Ignore them." When his eyes returned to hers, they lacked their previous urgency. "Sorry. I got a little carried away with myself. It's been a long day."

"Forget it. We'll see each other down the trail."

Breeze nodded. "Hope so. Guess you're going to bed now? Alone?"

"Gotten used to that. I kind of like it."

"Different strokes. You know where to find me if you change your mind."

Grace watched Breeze leave the enclosure with slow steps and disappear into one of the first floor rooms. The Sideways Seven dispersed. The other guests had gone. Grace looked at the flashing yellow neon of the '*Welcome—Vacancy*' sign. The hotel seemed deserted.

"If that had been Lone Star instead of Breeze…" She returned to her room lost in thought.

In the shower, the soft spray felt comforting. Warm water ran over her head and dripped into her open mouth until she was afraid the manager might knock on her door for running up the bill.

If only I could wash away some of this longing.

Afterward, she pulled back the orange striped bedspread and lay down on the crisp sheets with a sigh. But her mind still raced with thoughts of the Texan. She rose and refilled her pack with supplies from Celine's box.

I can get a head start tomorrow.

Close to midnight, she crawled back into bed but eventually rolled out her mat and sleeping bag on the carpet, unable to find a comfortable position on the soft mattress. The hard floor felt relaxing and familiar. She drifted off.

She woke at four.

Time to get out of here.

The starry sky framed the darkened windows of the other rooms.

Lone Star, here I come.

CHAPTER 16

After finishing the PCT's Mojave section, Grace ascended into the Sierra Nevada Mountains, the peaks that put *Crest* in PCT. The path still periodically descended to the desert, but it meandered more frequently through oak and pine forests, zigzagged up rocky faces, and sliced ridges with breathtaking vistas of distant mountains. She occasionally stepped in stride with a fellow thru or section hiker. But during the eight days until the next resupply stop at Kennedy Meadows, she primarily wanted time to herself.

If it can't be Lone Star, I don't want it to be anyone else.

A third of the way into the section between Mojave and Kennedy Meadows, the trail climbed above five thousand feet. From then on, it stayed there, a prelude to the real Sierras that began past Kennedy Meadows. The peaks and valleys on Grace's elevation profile tightened. The trail still lacked shade, the air continued to be hot, and it never rained. But this new environment offered water in more abundance.

When she reached Kennedy Meadows, she took a day off, her aching thighs demanding a rest.

Celine's resupply box that awaited her at the store held enough for twelve days. Grace stared at the contents of the heavy box.

I'll have to pull down at least sixteen miles a day, or I'll run out of food. Where's a donkey when I need one?

The store at Kennedy Meadows was a simple log cabin. But it boasted showers, a rarity on the trail. Grace paid the fee at the register, gathered her laundry, and headed out back. The shower stalls, rickety plywood boxes surrounding exposed water pipes, sat on a rise. Grace admired the cloudless sky as a week's worth of dirt ran off her and turned the water brown. Tree boughs swayed in the breeze. She shaved her legs for the first time in weeks and shampooed three times.

She called Celine while sitting under a tree near her tent, letting the warm sun dry her hair.

"I should be at Vermillion Valley Resort in two Saturdays, give or take."

"Did I send enough food to get you there?"

"You sent almost more than I can carry. I'll make it last."

"Can you resupply somewhere if you're desperate?"

"Not easily. This section's remote." She shook an ant from her leg. "Don't worry. I'm prepared. By now I think I know just about everything that could go wrong out here."

"Remember not to race anybody down a

mountain. I don't think that plays to your strengths."

They both laughed.

That evening, Grace joined the crowd on the store patio and scanned the assortment of hikers for unlikely combinations. Tanned young women in pastel shorts with sun-bleached blonde hair cascading from under ultralight hiking caps joked with disheveled men in ripped, grime bespattered shirts and boots that smelled like rotting skunks even from two tables away. Clean-shaven youth with crew cuts discussed water filtering with men whose matted hair and scruffy beards reached mid-chest. The air held odors of sweat, french fries, and sunscreen. The atmosphere exuded bonhomie.

On the crowded porch, only one man sat alone.

Breeze.

He leaned back on a plastic chair with his feet against the railing. A half-empty beer bottle lay propped against his chest. He gave Grace a long, indecipherable glance when she waved and approached his seat.

"Hi, Breeze."

"Hi, Grace." He looked from her and back to the meadow.

"Mind if I sit down?"

His lips twitched. "Suit yourself."

Grace pulled an unoccupied chair from the nearest table and joined him.

"Rescue anyone lately?"

He gave her an anemic smile. "Been too busy."

"With what?"

"This and that."

"Oh." She followed his gaze and fixed her eyes on the dry landscape.

He took a swig from his bottle. "Hiking any faster these days?"

"I've been pulling down some twenty-twos with these stubby legs. I'm pretty proud."

"That's decent."

"Sure." Grace gestured north. "But the real mountains are ahead of us."

"If you get into trouble, maybe I'll be around to help you out."

Grace grinned. "I'm trying to avoid those kinds of situations."

Breeze laid his hand on her thigh. "Maybe I can help you out in other ways?"

Grace pulled her leg gently from underneath his fingers. "I appreciate the thought. But the whole trail thing. All this anonymity. It's not sexy. At least not for me."

Breeze leaned in closer. "I'll tell you my name. If it makes a difference."

"You can try."

"It's Ed."

"Ed what?"

He looked around. His mouth brushed Grace's ear. "Ed Galeano."

The whisper's tickle made her shiver. She shrugged. "Sorry. Good try. But it doesn't quite work for me. Great to know I can find you again if I wanted to though."

Breeze's fingers gripped her leg. His narrowed eyes fixed on her with a coldness that contrasted sharply with the convivial chatter on the porch.

"Keep my name to yourself, okay? Out here, I'm Breeze. Get it?"

Grace regarded him quizzically and pushed back her chair. "Got it." She stood, yawned, and crossed her arms. Hikers were flocking to their tents in the deepening shadows. "It's getting cold. I'm going to call it a night."

Breeze nodded and turned back to the meadow.

***

In the fading afternoon light of the following day, Grace spread her pack's contents on the sandy ground by her tent and emptied Celine's box next to it. A mesh of triangular snow spikes glittered atop a pile of power bars. The prongs poked her legs as she fitted the metal cleats onto the bottom of her shoes.

People say it's a low snow year. I'd prefer a no snow year.

She stood up and walked a few steps, leaving futuristic footprints in the sand.

I guess they'll give me traction as long as it's not too deep.

The metal clinked and rattled when she shoved the set to the bottom of her pack.

With all that noise, at least the bears will know I'm coming.

She filled two stuff sacks with food.

Twelve days to Vermillion Valley Resort at Lake Edison. I hope I don't end up hating power bars.

The remaining items filled her pack to the gills. She cinched it shut, lifted it off the ground with a groan, and carried it to a nearby boulder. Her arms slipped through the straps and she bent forward.

Here goes nothing.

The pack balanced precariously on her back.

Ugh. This thing weighs more than Hope's twins after a Chuck E. Cheese party.

She straightened and fastened the waist belt.

Nothing to do but get used to this. Preferably out of sight.

She scanned the area.

Nobody.

Her feet traced a narrow oval around her tent while her mind willed strength to her shoulders. Cool gusts of air rushed intermittently through the pine boughs above her head. The scent of crushed needles filled her lungs.

She'd begun to hum the "The Happy Wanderer" when a familiar voice interrupted her meditation.

"Now there's a woman with some snap in her garters." The deep Texan drawl made her jump.

Her voice, when it recovered, quivered with equal parts disbelief and hope. "Lone Star?"

"None other."

Large hands gently turned her around, sparking a flood of longing that rushed from her toes to her scalp.

Strong arms enfolded her and Grace melted into the embrace, forgetting to breathe. Fingers stroked her face. Soft lips pressed against hers. She leaned her cheek into each caress, choking back a moan as Lone Star murmured apologies into her ear. Her fists clenched his shirt like she would never let go.

"How did you find me?"

"Never mind that now."

Lone Star kissed her with a passion fueled by weeks of yearning. His eyes darkened and then closed against the rapidly growing twilight. Grace stood on tiptoe as he leaned over her and angled his head to probe deeper. Her mouth opened wider, welcoming the exploration. His touch felt both exhilarating and supremely comfortable. Her eyes roamed over his long lashes and square forehead. She ran her hands again and again through his thick red hair.

I never want this to end.

Too soon, he released his grip and pushed her from him. She disengaged with the reluctance of a suction cup and balanced, breathing heavily, on unsteady legs.

"I don't want to stop."

"I can hardly get my arms around you properly, Just Grace, with that pack on your back."

He stepped behind, lifted it from her shoulders, and leaned it against a tree.

"Funny. I forgot I was wearing it."

"Funny what love will do."

Her stomach jumped.

Love?

Before her thoughts continued, Lone Star's hands clasped her rear and pulled her body against the firm plane of his chest. Grace wiggled closer, trying to eliminate areas where their torsos didn't make contact. She reached for his hips, drawing them toward her. At the same time, surprisingly soft hands slid under her shirt and up her firm stomach until they each cupped a warm breast in a protective embrace.

His rough chin nuzzled into the recess below her collar bone. His lips covered her neck and jaw with kisses. A soft murmur escaped her as she turned her head to give him better access.

When his lips tugged her breast, her skin, electrified, jumped from a slow simmer to a sudden boil.

"I'm too hot." She gasped, stepped away, and pulled her shirt over her head.

Lone Star chuckled. "You *are* hot, Just Grace. But easy does it. We've got lots of time."

"No, seriously." She pulled away from him. "I'm burning up." She threw her shirt heedlessly over her shoulder and stepped out of her shorts.

"Grace. You're more beautiful than I imagined. And I imagined a lot."

"Like how the pulsing joy you shared with me lifts you to the sky?"

"Like how I want you to *fold thyself, my dearest, and slip into my bosom and be lost in me*."

"Oh, Lone Star. That's the kind of Texas romance I missed all these weeks."

Lone Star lifted her into his arms and carried her to the tent.

***

Late that evening they lay together, his body wrapped tightly around hers. The reassurance of the past few hours, the parallels of their yearning, speed, and tenderness, made Grace's limbs heavier with satisfaction than they had been in years.

"Hey." She nudged him drowsily.

"What?" He traced the outline of her forehead with his fingers.

"I never even asked you what happened. Why you stopped leaving me notes."

Lone Star stroked her hair and burrowed his head into her neck. Grace missed his reply as she drifted to sleep.

CHAPTER 17

Voices woke her the following morning.

Her head rode the tide of Lone Star's deep breathing as she lay on his chest and blinked the sleep from her eyes. She matched their inhalations and twined her legs more tightly around his.

Last night was like a volcanic eruption. My shirt and shorts were so in the way.

Her eyes popped open.

My clothes.

She searched her memory.

They're hanging on a bush. And Lone Star's are…over a tree branch. Great. Your basic lingerie display. Perfect for thrus on their way to breakfast.

She disentangled herself gently. Her camp shoes were in the sleeping bag stuff sack at the other end of the tent. She extracted them carefully.

Her eyes peeped through a small opening in the tent zipper.

Coast is clear. Now or never.

She flung her yellow camp shoes out the flap and darted naked into the open. Goose pimples sprouted on her arms and legs in the frigid morning air. She scanned the surroundings.

There they are.

Her shirt clung to the branches of a blueberry bush. She ripped it free. Her shorts laid in a limp lump on the ground. She rushed toward them. An appreciative whistle issued from the trail. She scooped her shorts and pulled her shirt over her head.

"Nice show."

Grace whipped around but saw no one.

"Hey." Lone Star poked his head out of the tent. "Quiet out there. Some of us are trying to get our beauty rest."

"It's not me making all the noise." She returned to the tent, squatted, and kissed Lone Star's red head. "I had an audience."

He laughed and pulled her ankle. Grace fell backward, giggling. He tugged her legs hand over hand while her bare bottom scraped a sandy track along the ground.

In the tent, he kissed her, then lifted the shirt over her head.

"I just put that on."

"Shush." He kissed her again, rubbing the bare skin of his chest against hers. "I'm preventing the inevitable. When I kiss you, you beg me to take off your clothes."

She licked his ear and tugged at his earlobe. "What did you say about heat in the desert? Hot as the hinges of hell?"

"You betcha."

"Well, that's how you make me feel, Lone Star.

Hot as the hinges of hell. Nobody's managed that before."

"Maybe they weren't trying hard enough."

The raw hunger of his embrace startled her. She rocked forward, deeper into his arms, and straddled his thighs as he crouched on the tent floor. Soft caresses floated over her neck and ear. Her fingers massaged his temples, his arms. They moved across his chest. Down his tight belly.

He groaned and leaned forward, easing her onto the sleeping bag. His body hovered over hers. The heat between them felt palpable. Lone Star gazed deep into Grace's eyes until she pulled him down, breathless. The moment stretched, and the outside world became lost in the perfectly synchronized rhythm of their desire.

Grace emerged an hour later and handed Lone Star his clothing through the flap. The sun stood well over the horizon. A constant stream of thrus passed the tent.

"I'm starving." She watched him pull on his shoes. "But I want to take another shower before I do anything else." Her small towel snapped as she flung it around her neck. "You go to the store. I'll meet you on the porch."

"I'll grab us breakfast." Lone Star planted a firm kiss on her lips. "Any requests?"

"Anything huge and fattening. And I could sure use a cup of coffee. Lots of cream. A ton of sugar."

"One deluxe hiker feast coming right up." He jogged toward the store, Grace watching the fabric of his shorts stretch over his lean frame as he ran.

His name.

"Wait. Lone Star." She dashed after him and, panting, grabbed both his hands. "I can't let you go anywhere without knowing."

"Knowing what, darlin'? I'll tell you anything."

"Your name."

"I never told you my name?"

"No. And the whole time on the trail I was terrified I'd never find you again."

"Aw, honey. There was no need to be scared. I'd have found you no matter where you were, faster than a sneeze through a screen door. But for the record, I'm Angus Hogan. Gus for short. Pleased to know you."

He pumped her hand. In the warm morning sunshine his red hair shone like a glowing ember. She clasped him to her and laughed.

Twenty minutes later, clean and smelling of peppermint, Grace sauntered up to Lone Star, who sat on a porch bench.

"Hey, Gus." She sat down beside him. "That doesn't sound right. I've been calling you Lone Star for weeks." Her fingers stroked his as she took the cup of coffee.

Lone Star plopped a bag in her lap. "Two chocolate muffins and a cream cheese strudel for my hungry lady. As far as I'm concerned, you can call me Gilligan's Island. If it comes out of your mouth, I'll answer to it."

Grace beamed and bit into a muffin. She pointed at it and gave a thumbs-up. "Delicious." Crumbs spewed onto Lone Star's lap. "Want some?"

"I already ate half a horse while waiting for you to get tidied up."

"I feel like I haven't eaten in a week." Grace wiped the back of her hand across her mouth.

"So you eat. I'll talk."

"Okay. Tell me again what happened. Why didn't I hear from you after the hiker register in Big Bear City? I fell asleep last night before you got to the punch line." Grace began her second muffin.

"It's not the kind of story to impress a lady. But here goes. Right before Big Bear City, there's a section where you have to walk along a ridge. Kind of precarious. Nothing most people can't handle. A lot of loose rock, with a steep drop to one side."

Grace nodded.

"Well, I lost my footing. I'd like to say I was daydreaming about you. But the reality is that I was dreaming of a Snickers bar. Good old Vitamin S. I'd eaten my last one a couple days before and was feeling mighty hungry right about then. I wasn't looking where I was going. I took one misstep and went head over heels down the ridge."

Grace almost choked on a bloated raisin. "The helicopter." She coughed out the offending morsel. "I remember hearing stories about someone being helicoptered out. Was that you?"

"I had the feeling you might hear about it. I was worried you might think it was me."

"Why would I think that?"

He took her hand and held it against his heart. "Because I was thinking of you the whole time. Every story I heard about a woman coming from behind, there was a second when I thought it might be about you."

"I did the same. But not for *that* story. I thought

176

it was an inexperienced newbie making a stupid mistake. Someone like me, not you. What happened?" She looked him up and down. "From what I saw last night and this morning, you've got all your working parts."

"That I do." His grin spanned from ear to ear. "I don't think I was ever as bad as I looked. But I looked pretty bad they said. All tore up. And unconscious. Happens that an Italian vet saw me take the header."

"A vet?"

"Veterinarian. She had an emergency beacon her husband made her take. Later, she came to the hospital to check on me. Said my fall made her reconsider hiking by herself. I think she said her husband was flying in and they were going back out together."

Grace was pale. "Oh my god, Lone Star." The half-finished danish lay untouched in her lap.

"Eat up, darling. You need to shovel as many calories as you can into that pretty mouth of yours."

"But you could have been killed."

He stood behind her and massaged her shoulders. "Tried to hang myself but the rope broke."

"Nobody's happier about that than me."

"You and my momma."

"Oh, of course." She craned her neck to look at him. "Did you go back to El Paso?"

"My folks flew up to stay while I was in the hospital. They rented a minivan to get me back home. It showed me how scared they were, spending money like that. My dad's usually tighter than a wet boot."

"They must have been sick with worry."

"I felt terrible leaving you in California. It felt like that old Cary Grant movie. Can't remember the name. The one where he's supposed to meet the lady at the top of the Empire State Building and she never shows up because she got hit by a car on the way."

"So I'm Cary Grant?"

"You've got the dark hair. I think the lady had red hair. So I fit that part better anyway."

"So how did you find me out here?"

"For that you can thank Celine."

"Celine?"

Lone Star tapped his forehead. "My terrific memory for details."

"I mentioned her?"

"You told me all about her. And about your psychology practice. And, don't forget, I knew your real name. So when your office wouldn't give me any information, I started digging around for Celine. Who'd have thought that her bank would be more likely to give out information about its employees than the psychologists in your group practice?"

"Yay for capitalism." Grace pulled him back to his seat. "I want to hear more. But I'm going to get a couple more muffins for the road. You want some too?"

Lone Star shook his head. "You go. When you come back, I've got a proposal for you."

The plastic chair buckled underneath her as she sat back down. The Ziploc baggie of credit cards and cash dropped to the floor.

"A proposal?" The chatter of hikers around them almost drowned her words.

Lone Star bent to retrieve the baggie. "You want to hear it now, before you eat?"

Grace's heart pounded and she felt like she'd struggled up the last leg of a steep mountain ascent. "Now."

He held out the bag. "You look whiter than Tom Sawyer's fence, Just Grace. You feeling okay after all that sugar?"

"Sugar's not the issue, Lone Star. You said you wanted to make me a proposal."

"Oh." Lone Star's cheeks outshone his red hair. "That's the attorney in me. We make proposals all the time. Motions. Proposals. Briefs. What I meant was…I had an idea."

The smile dropped from Grace's eyes.

"Not that…well…not that those kinds of thoughts haven't crossed my mind, darlin'. But I told myself I was nuts. I mean, we just met. If I said anything like that, well, you'd think I was two sandwiches short of a picnic."

"I wouldn't. You've been with me practically every step of this trail. I've jumped far into the future with you many times."

"Heck, Just Grace, I have too. But I don't even know if you've got a boyfriend back home."

"Lone Star, there's one thing you can rely on. I don't cheat on people. My last boyfriend was Ben. He and I broke up over a year ago."

"So we're both unattached."

Grace looked into his blue eyes. "I don't feel unattached."

"Neither do I. Proposals may be premature. But I'm going to give this all I've got."

Grace moved onto Lone Star's lap. The plastic underneath them groaned as she showered his face with tiny kisses. "You've already got all I've got, Lone Star."

After a few minutes, she pushed herself off him. "Now that we've got that out of the way, I know you'll stay put until I come back with my muffins."

When she returned, Lone Star greeted her with a hug then held her at arm's length. "We never got to my idea. I told my colleagues I'd only be gone two days. We've got a big case going on. But right now, here with you, I don't care. They can manage without me. So if you're willing to take another zero, I'll rebook my flight and stay here till tomorrow morning."

"Willing?" Grace jumped into his arms. "I'd already planned to tie you down with my bear rope if you said you were leaving."

"Good thing I changed my mind, then." He twirled her hair around his fingers as she snuggled into his chest. "Now that we have the whole day ahead of us, how do you suggest we spend our time?"

Grace pulled him off the porch in the direction of her tent.

"You've changed, Just Grace," Lone Star said as she pushed him inside.

"What do you mean?"

"You've got more spunk. You know your own mind. When I found you out there in the desert, you were searching."

"Now I've found what I want?" Her hands stroked his inner thighs.

A chuckle rumbled in his chest. "Not only that. As much as I'd like to take the credit, I think you did this on your own."

She resumed her exploration of his shorts. "What they call 'trail magic'?"

"What they call 'hiking your own hike.'" He removed her hand. "Let me take the lead, my love. Nice and slow this time. Texas style."

With the speed and artistry of a potter working a piece of clay, Lone Star separated Grace from her clothing. He caressed, kneaded, and stroked her torso. Kissed her eyes. Cradled her head in one of his large hands while maneuvering the other under the backs of her knees.

"I thought you did things big in Texas."

He lifted her nude body off the ground and stretched it on the nylon, tucking her clothes behind her head as a pillow.

"Big doesn't have to mean fast, Just Grace."

She watched him languorously unbutton his shirt and giggled. "I feel like I'm at a male strip show."

He pulled off his shorts, long and slow, one leg at a time. Then he nestled his head onto her abdomen and curled his legs beside hers.

"In Texas, cooking a good barbecued brisket can take all day."

"Well, we've got…" A quick inhalation of breath sucked the words out of her mouth as Lone Star's lips brushed past her belly button and began to explore the region below.

***

Lone Star left the next morning after breakfast, hitching a ride with the father of a northbound thru. Grace's heart felt light.

He loves me.

Her body tingled with renewed energy and her feet itched to begin walking.

I could sail across these mountains. The faster I go, the sooner I'll see him again.

At ten, she left the sandy turf for Kennedy Meadows Campground. Ahead lay a kaleidoscope of peaks, fords, and lakes, beginning with the trail's highest point, Forester Pass. Then up and down over Glen, Pinchot, Mather, Muir, and Selden Passes.

Only squirrels and crows accompanied Grace to the campsites near the Kern River. As she passed the empty tenting spots, a voice called from the direction of the water.

"Hey! We could use some help over here."

Grace looked around. A young blonde waved frantically from the middle of the river. Grace looked behind her. "Me?"

"Yes, you. Can you help us out?"

The tall grasses tickled her bare legs as Grace pushed toward the gentle rushing of the water. When she got closer, she saw more people, all in t-shirts and shorts, standing knee deep in the flowing stream.

"Thanks." The woman motioned to her friends when Grace reached the bank. "We're having a contest, and we need a judge. A fair judge." Her words slurred.

"How can I help?"

One of the men spoke up. "We're having a problem with cheating." Before he could continue, a friend shoved him from behind. He lost his balance and fell to his knees in the water.

The standing friend clarified. "Only *one* of us has been cheating…" Two men stopped him in mid-explanation by showering him with river water until he gagged.

Grace pointed to the remaining woman, a brunette who stood apart from the water fight. Her shoulder-length hair was tied back with a pink bandana. Sweat stains encircled the underarms and neckline of a floral t-shirt, and her mauve running shorts were patched with material in the shape of a heart. Despite the worn clothing and grime, Grace recognized the remainders of a thru-hiker fashionista.

Maybe she'll have a more sensible attitude.

"You in the flowered t-shirt. Yes, you. Tell me what you want me to do."

The brunette gave her friends a smug smile. Hands on her hips, she thrust out her chest so that it strained the thinning fabric.

"Well, we were having a little drink at the store this morning." She enunciated her words with effort. "And Gordon here was talking about how he can do this awesome handstand. To make a long story…I mean, a short…we thought Gordon was full of shit. But to make things interesting, we moved it to the river."

The woman stared at Grace.

"Moved *what* to the river?"

"The contest." The woman sighed. "Don't you get it?"

This is like talking to a two-year-old.

"What *kind* of contest?"

"Oh, didn't I say? A handstand contest. We all do a handstand in the river. And whoever stays up longest wins." The woman threw out her arms to emphasize the last word and wobbled. One of her friends caught her before she hit the water.

"Easy there, Ecstasy." He took over. "You didn't tell her the problem. The problem is that when we're all upside down, we can't see anything. Like if somebody," he pointed at the man he'd shoved earlier, "comes up for air in between."

"Dude, who're you accusing of cheating?" The first man, still kneeling in the river with the current eddying around his legs, struggled to stand.

"Hey, back off, you two." Grace clapped her hands. "I don't want to be here all day. I get it. I'll be the judge. I'll give the word, and you start. Ready?"

"Wait." The second man held up his hand. "You gotta know our names. How else can you choose the winner?"

"That's right." Grace frowned. "Silly me. I couldn't just point to one of you."

"Straight up. We might not know who you're pointing at. I'm Bud." He slapped his chest and turned to the man on his left.

"I'm Gordon."

"I'm Stoli."

"I'm Bacardi."

"I'm Southern Comfort."

"I'm Margie."

"And I'm Ecstasy."

I finally get to put names to the faces of the Sideways Seven.

"So let's get this show on the road." Grace took a step closer to the bank.

The group spread across the riverbed, arms held high.

Grace shouted through cupped hands, "Ready...go."

Each of the Seven pitched forward and fourteen legs thrust straight into the air.

I'll give this contest about five seconds.

Toes pointed to the sky like a row of upside down lizards. No one moved.

Grace counted. "One one thousand, two one thousand, three one thousand..."

When she reached twenty-seven one thousand, Margie's legs swayed. At thirty-one one thousand, she tipped over backward and sat in the water, sputtering. Bud was the next down. Then Gordon, Southern Comfort, and Bacardi in rapid succession. Then the six spectators watched as Stoli and Ecstasy passed Grace's one minute mark and kept going.

"Told you tit size has something to do with lung size." Gordon nudged Bacardi. But Bacardi didn't respond. His eyes were fixed on the couple in the water.

Grace continued counting. The silence was reverential.

In the end, Ecstasy's legs shook. At one and thirteen one thousand, she crashed into the water, sending up a shower that made Grace retreat from the sandy bank. Stoli's legs remained ramrod straight until after Ecstasy fell, and then, as if hooked to a spring, he curled his legs to his chest and bounced out of the water, flipping to his feet like an Olympian.

He shook water from his hair like a dog. "Did I win?"

Grace stepped to the edge of the water and reached out her hand to congratulate him. "Stoli's the winner." She raised his arm. "One minute sixteen seconds. The grand water handstander of the PCT."

Stoli laughed. "Four fucking years of gymnastics in high school finally paid off." He splashed a victory circle through the shallows to the applause of his friends and waved his arms about his head and hollered. "Milwaukee's good for something after all."

CHAPTER 18

Grace had hiked consistent twenty-two mile days in the past weeks. In the Sierras she only managed seventeen. The elevation profile graphs spiked. Drops were abbreviated, like an S-wave from a seismograph. The trail ascended from river valleys and soared toward passes. Mountain peaks towered on either side as the path crested divides and then plunged toward valley bottoms. Climbing with extra food was taxing. But what slowed her down the most was the snow.

Snowfields were as barren and dangerous as the desert had been. And snow had peculiarities all its own. It could obscure tread, signposts, cairns, and landmarks. Under extreme conditions, what looked like a flat, empty terrain could in reality be a forest.

Snow was erratic, fickle. Where the snow line started on a mountain depended on the elevation and the angle of the sun. North faces had more snow than south faces. As the summer progressed, more snow melted. Its reach changed constantly.

Neither was all white stuff equal. Its consistency

depended on the time of day. And consistency was everything.

Hard pack snow, Grace soon learned, was her friend. The herd of thrus wore a discolored path that the metal spikes attached to her running shoes gripped reassuringly. A makeshift staircase stomped into frozen snow didn't collapse under her weight. But on south-facing valley walls in mid-afternoon the snow had the consistency of a Slurpee. She slid one step back for two forward.

So Grace began each day at first light, when subfreezing temperatures solidified the white landscape. That was when experienced thrus skied down snow-covered slopes on their boots, expertly gliding and twisting as though they had boards strapped to their feet.

The best Grace could do was slide on her behind. But she stopped doing that after she collided with a partially submerged rock. Afterward, she couldn't sit for a day. From then on, she walked downhill sideways when she could, and backwards when she had to.

I don't intend to repeat my dramatic mountain tumble.

Above the tree line, metallic chirps of marmots and ground squirrels broadcast her arrival. Flowers hugged the terrain alongside boulders the size of cars. Vast granite cliffs cut across the blue sky. She looked down on verdant valleys and deep, dark blue lakes where delicate patterns of snow and ice crisscrossed the surfaces. Often, as elevations increased, the setting reminded her of a quarry. Acres of rocks stretched in front of her, with some stones smaller than a frog and others larger than houses. All blended to form a rough, integrated surface.

Like pictures I've seen of the moon.

Thoughts of Lone Star accompanied her as the days progressed. His strong, nurturing presence blended seamlessly with the majesty of the landscape. She sometimes imagined climbing to the top of a pass to find him sitting on a rock.

Don't rush it. He'll be at VVR with a room reserved and a Dallas-size meal and bed waiting for me. Like he quoted in the tent: "License my roving hands, and let them go. Before, behind, between, above, below."

Lone Star. I license all your parts.

Getting to Pinchot Pass required threading numerous tributaries of Woods Creek. As she crossed the first, she heard a familiar whooping. When she reached dry land, she turned to watch. One by one, the Sideways Seven skittered along the trail at breakneck speed and flung themselves across the water headlong, hurtling from one boulder to another. Ecstasy led the group. When she reached Grace's side, she stopped.

"Hey, dudes, it's the handstand judge." The seven hikers gathered. Grace recognized Margie, the only other woman, and Stoli, with his floppy hair and lithe, gymnast build. But to her, the rest of the men were indistinguishable.

"Any more contests?"

"'Course." Stoli put his hand in his pocket. "What would a day be without a contest? We're trying to see who will last the longest on M&Ms."

He pulled out a multi-colored handful. The candy glistened in the sun before he shoveled it into his mouth. "I'm gonna win this one too." He gave her a chocolatey smile.

"You're eating nothing but M&Ms?"

"They're peanut. They're good for you." Margie's voice held no trace of irony.

Grace shot her an incredulous glance. "Right. I'm sure they're much higher on the food pyramid."

"We've gone two and a half days so far. No one's caved yet."

"What about alcohol? Does that count against you?" Grace winked at Stoli.

"Hell, no. It's strictly about food. With all this nature around, you've got to get sideways whenever you can." He drew another handful of M&Ms from his pocket and offered it to Grace. "Want some?"

She stared at the mixture.

How long have those been in his pants? Oh, what the heck.

The sweet hulls crunched as her teeth sunk into delightfully warm chocolate and crisp, salty peanuts. "Spectacular."

Others in the group fished out their stashes. "Here. Take more." Soon Grace's pockets overflowed with M&M donations.

"Thanks for refereeing back at the creek." Stoli gave her a quick nod as the group pushed on through the trees. "That was the first time in my life I ever won anything."

Later, at the top of Pinchot Pass, Grace sat on a rocky outcropping, munched half-melted M&Ms, and looked at her map. Rocks and boulders dotted the dry terrain around her. High ridges and peaks scalloped the horizon. Snowcapped mountains towered miles ahead. Tufts of white clouds floated across the azure sky.

I'll camp at the Bench Lake trail junction in the valley. The wind up here could keep me awake all night.

When she arrived at Bench Lake near dusk, the dimming light illuminated a pair of fishermen casting for bites on the opposite shore. She wolfed down a cold dinner, put all her extra food into her new bear canister, and on an afterthought, jammed her shorts in as well.

Black bear country. Don't want a roving prowler to sniff out the M&M residue.

She hung the container from a distant tree branch, crawled into her tent, and stroked the yellow walls.

This thin fabric won't stop a bear. Or even a determined mouse. But it's my fortress in the wilderness.

An owl hooted. Two raccoons scuffled through the brush.

I'm in one of the most peaceful places on earth. It can't get any better than this.

CHAPTER 19

Grace awoke the next morning to the sound of a man's voice echoing over the lake.

Lone Star?

She sat up.

There it is again.

She peered out but couldn't see anyone in the strong morning light. She shrugged.

He'll be amused when I tell him I hear his voice in the trees.

The day's hiking brought more river fordings. Grace's pace slowed the steep, zigzagging ascent to Mather Pass.

At the top of the pass, fourteen thousand-foot mountains pierced an endless sky. Northern harriers circled on thermals. She picked a rock for an early lunch and afterward tightened her pack straps to prevent swaying on the knee-breaking, gravity-assisted descent on the infamous Golden Staircase.

***

Fifteen miles ahead of her, the sun was still high in the sky when the Sideways Seven settled in for a rest. They had cruised up and down Pinchot and Mather Passes the day before, and that morning had predicted pulling down at least twenty miles. But their plans took a sudden turn after they ran into a group of horse packers at Little Pete Meadow.

The Seven knew a pack animal meant alcohol. They pulled worn ten and five dollar bills from plastic baggies and waved them at the passing riders, who jerked their horses to a stop and negotiated steep prices for beer and hard liquor. With enough booze to last them well into the night, the Seven started drinking before their packs hit the ground.

They sat in a flattened circle of crushed meadow grass. Bottles of beer, vodka, and gin passed from mouth to mouth. Stoli leaned against a rough pine log, using a twig to poke carpenter ants excavating a burl. Whenever one emerged from the hole carrying a piece of bark, Stoli flicked it into the grass with a laugh. "Better luck next time."

Bud and Bacardi lay on their stomachs and dozed. Southern Comfort rolled a can between rough palms and hummed an ad-libbed version of *Beer, Beer, Beer*. Others joined in.

In the early afternoon, their voices wafted across the green meadow and into the nearby woods, frightening curious deer.

***

Breeze woke earlier that same day, not far

behind Grace. He had spent an uncomfortable night at the top of Pinchot Pass and now hiked at full speed to gain warmth and time. The night at Pinchot had been the worst of his hike, and he kicked savagely at small rocks that flew in all directions like scattershot. He'd lost his headlamp, nearly lost his tent, and now directed his foul humor at Jerry.

That bastard is probably miles ahead at some grassy campsite, getting wasted with his friends. I've been out here almost seven weeks, and I've never caught him alone. What kind of sitting duck goes around with six fricking bodyguards? High time I stop caring. Time to go after him, alone or not.

It was still early as he, muttering loudly, passed close to the edge of the lake where Grace's tent was set up out of sight. At mid-morning, he reached the top of Mather Pass.

Grace, by that point, was a few hours behind him on the trail.

And twelve miles ahead, at Little Pete Meadow, Jerry was getting wasted with his friends.

CHAPTER 20

That day, the Golden Staircase descent wore Grace out, so she chose to rest her aching legs at Le Conte Canyon, well before Little Pete Meadow.

After a quick dinner, her head lay on the sack of rolled up clothing. She replayed a frequent internal monologue she called "When this hike is over."

When this hike is over, I'll go back to San Francisco—to freeways and rush hour traffic, clients in crisis, work email on my iPhone, mortgage payments, staff meetings, yoga wait lists, and forty-minute stress reduction workouts at the gym. The off-trail life that used to seem so easy. Now it feels so hard. And where does Lone Star fit in? Out here, there's room for him. But how do big hands, an El Paso law practice, and dust storms align with short legs, psychotherapy, and fog? We'll have to work it out. But it sure is easier here, with a tent, some food, and a heck of a lot of peace.

Before first light, a shower of needles peppered her shelter like soft rain. Birds twittered in the branches overhead. Grace disassembled her tent in the darkness, the tent poles snapping easily back into their sections. She rolled the ground cloth into a tight bundle, careful not to include any sand or gravel, stuffed her camp shoes in with her sleeping bag, and stowed the remainder of her gear. When the sun rose above the horizon, she walked to Dusy Branch Creek, filtered water into two bottles, and set out for Muir Pass.

She saw no other hikers until she passed Little Pete Meadow. There, two tents, each with a pair of shoes at the entrance, occupied opposite ends of the narrow field.

I wonder who's sleeping late.

She passed quietly as screeching hawks circled, looking for prey in the grass.

When she reached Muir Pass and a beehive-shaped stone hut, the east slopes were covered in snow.

Thank goodness I started early.

She pulled on spikes and followed the frozen footsteps of countless previous hikers. The ascent felt easy at first. But as it progressed, weariness from the previous day set in again. By mid-afternoon, Grace felt her thirty-four years. The sun still glinted high in the summer sky when she reached Evolution Creek.

Seventeen miles so far. That's a record for me in the Sierras.

She looked at her map.

I'll get to the campsites near the Hell for Sure Pass Trail. Then I've had it for the day.

The "creek" was wide. She searched for a reasonable place to cross. Skeletal pine trees towered between boulders, shadowing the low grass at the water's edge.

She chose a spot far above a narrows where the creek cascaded over several ledges in a series of waterfalls. The foam camp shoes she pulled from her sleeping bag sack floated in the shallows while she tied the laces of her hiking shoes together and cinched them under the compression straps of her pack. Icy snow runoff washed over her ankles as she stepped into the water.

Only two seconds in and my feet feel like ice cubes.

Avoiding slippery rocks, she eased her way across the stream. The water rose to her knees and she needed her hiking poles to remain upright. The surging force increased its grip as she moved, one careful step at a time until, halfway across, the creek reached her waist. Each time she looked down into the torrent, she gasped from dizziness.

Look straight ahead. Keep moving.

Grace shivered as she approached the shore. Water dripped from the pack. Wet shorts clung to her goose bump-covered legs.

At least I didn't fall in.

With the water still mid-thigh, she wrung out the legs of her shorts. There was something hard in one of her pockets.

My phone.

Her fingers tore it out of the pocket with such violence that she lost her balance. She fell head first into the creek.

The weight of her pack pinned her down. River water filled her mouth.

After a panicked struggle, she flipped to her knees. Coughing and spitting, she clawed her way up the bank and fell panting on the grass. Her hand still clutched the phone.

She pushed buttons.

No response. She cradled the black rectangle against her face.

My entire hike wiped out. All because I forgot to put it back in the plastic baggie. I have to try to dry it out.

She spotted stone ledges near the waterfalls, a hundred feet downstream, and ran. At the rocks, she dumped the contents of her pack and searched for something dark in color.

She spread phone, battery, and SIM card on the navy nylon of her sleeping bag.

Now I'll wait.

Water droplets on the black phone case glittered reproachfully in the sun. She shivered from fear and agitation.

You're not hurt, Grace. Your hiking shoes are dry. This could've been a lot worse.

Small waterfalls gurgled below. The scent of warm pine needles reminded her of peaceful hours on the trail. Surrounding peaks towered, imposing and untroubled.

But her stomach felt like she'd swallowed a ball of ice. The breeze cooled her wet clothing. Her teeth chattered.

I should get out of these clothes.

A search of her pack resulted in only two completely dry items: a pair of socks and a bandana.

She looked around.

Nobody.

Her wet clothing joined the cell phone parts in the sun. She scrubbed her body with the bandana and lay down on the rock, nude, gear scattered around her like a mosaic. She closed her eyes.

I'll be dry before anyone comes.

CHAPTER 21

Earlier that same day, Stoli awoke in his tent at Little Pete Meadow to the sensation of hair growing inside his mouth. As he slowly ran his tongue across the dry landscape of his palate, he tried to remember the night before.

What happened?

He made out the world through the tiny slit that was his left eye. The right lid wouldn't budge. His fingers gingerly explored puffy skin.

Ouch. Two black eyes?

He lay back and groaned. But the fur in his mouth tickled. He rubbed his head and pushed himself upright. Something heavy fell in his lap. An arm lay between his legs.

Mine?

He poked at it, hefted it with difficulty, and let it flop to the ground.

Must be asleep. Guess I had too much to drink.

The strong morning sunlight assaulted his working eye as he crawled through the tent entrance, dragging his useless arm behind him. He dug one-handed in his pack and took a deep pull from a water bottle.

Ugh. Vodka.

He spat it out, searched again, and found a collapsible container. He sniffed.

Doesn't smell like vodka.

He sipped carefully.

Water.

He downed the contents and took his filter in search of more, stumbling across the uneven field. Tall grass brushed against his bare legs, triggering memories of the previous day's activities.

Yesterday started to look up when we ran into the horse packers. Yeah. That was a find. We set up camp right here.

He looked around him at the trampled grass.

So where's everyone? We were drinking. Started around eleven. Right before that other hiker joined us. The one with the whiskey-filled water bottle. Never liked whiskey. But booze is booze. He shared. What was his name? Freeze? Something like that.

So where did things go wrong?

The poker.

***

That night, the Seven had broken out a pack of cards and started playing strip poker for a little fun, like always. The game was Stoli's favorite, and despite his friends always making him start with a penalty, he was usually the one with his clothes on at the end.

The game started out as usual. Breeze, who had

approached the group around noon, joined in. Margie and Ecstasy quickly lost their shoes, socks, and shorts. Only caps and shoes hit the pile from the men's side. Stoli frequenly won. But his mind wasn't on the game. He was watching Ecstasy, bothered that she was ignoring him.

Do I turn her off? Is she mad I slept with Margie? Everyone's slept with Margie. I think even Ecstasy slept with her.

But now Ecstasy's hooked up with Gordon. They got together right after that bear incident—a sympathy lay. At least that's what it looked like. But they keep at it hot and heavy.

What's Gordon got I don't? Stupid asshole. Likes to show off. Rubs Ecstasy in my face. Ever since the first time he laid her.

At the game, Margie was the first to lose all her clothes. She staggered to her tent, clothes in hand, too drunk to remember to put them back on. Southern Comfort then stampeded to last place, preoccupied with Margie. He cheated, and the others took his shorts. He ran straight to Margie's tent, hands between his legs.

As the others cheered Southern Comfort on, Stoli glimpsed Gordon wink at Ecstasy and pretend to throw in his cards. Ecstasy licked her lips.

When the game recommenced, Ecstasy lost hand after hand until she stood naked, scooped up her belongings, flashed Gordon a smile, and headed to her tent.

Someone in the remaining group called a bathroom break and everyone spread out, except Stoli. He watched Gordon run after Ecstasy, kiss her on the lips, and cup her breasts in his hands.

"Hang tight." He gave them a squeeze. "I'll be the next one out."

He makes me sick.

The group reconvened and the game resumed, Stoli losing as skillfully as he usually won, his penalty giving him a head start to the finish. He was undressed before any of the others knew what had happened.

"I'm hitting the sack. See you in the morning." He sulked toward his tent, stumbling deliberately to seem more drunk than he felt. He crawled inside, waited a minute, then poked his head through the flap, squinting at the circle of moving lights around the game.

Tonight I'll get to Ecstasy before Gordon does.

The nearly full moon cast shadows. He pulled on his shorts and boots and walked carefully, heel to toe, bent low to the ground, making a wide circle around the remaining players through the surrounding field. The scratchy grass tickled his chest. He periodically glanced back toward the game, but all the lights stayed put.

He reached Ecstasy's tent and pulled the flap aside. She was snoring. He dropped his shorts on his boots and snuck inside.

There was little light, but what there was illuminated her naked body stretched atop a sleeping bag.

Stoli rested on his knees. His heart pounded, body stiff as a rock. He stroked her calf and his fingers trembled. He ran his hands farther up her body, feeling silky dark hair, a soft depression, and smooth hips. Nipples rose at his touch and he pinched them.

She wants me. What a body. How can I control myself when she looks like that?

He pinched the nipples harder. Ecstasy moaned.

"Shhh."

He inched closer and put his hand over her mouth. Her tongue licked his thumb, pulled it between her lips, and sucked.

Christ. She wants me to give it to her.

Pushing her legs apart, he fell between her knees, breathing hard, ears thundering, body shaking.

He pushed.

"Jesus."

Just before his member entered her, a hand tore at his shoulder, ripping him backward and flinging him outside in one smooth arc.

"What the fuck do you think you're doing?"

Stoli recognized Gordon a split second before he felt a punch to his eye.

"You fucking loser."

Gordon landed a hard kick to Stoli's ribs that sent him rolling across the grass. Then he disappeared inside the tent.

Beams of light bounced across the meadow. Gordon threw Stoli's shorts and boots at him, one boot glancing off Stoli's cheek.

"Get out of here before I kill you."

Stoli shoved feet into boots and bolted across the meadow, shorts in hand, to a clump of large boulders. The lights followed.

"Leave me alone." He shivered behind the rocks. "I didn't do anything. Nothing happened."

The lights kept coming.

He found a hiding place and pulled on his shorts, watching the headlamp beams swing over the area around the tent. Stoli sprinted to the bordering woods for cover.

The lights hunted him for hours. He dodged beams flickering in the pines. Bark and brush scratched his legs as he ran. Mosquitos swarmed. Beer and whiskey played with his sense of direction.

What do they want? It was no big deal. I never really touched her.

Hiding in dark corners of the wood, he jogged in place to keep warm and keep away the bugs. He wanted to sneak back to camp, but one persistent light still shone in the darkness.

Who's that jerk who won't give up? Probably Gordon. But what's he trying to prove? Ecstasy would have been happy to wake up with me on top of her. Yeah, that's it. I'm his competition and he wants to get rid of me.

It was almost dawn when Stoli saw a second light and heard voices. A few minutes later, the beams disappeared. He waited half an hour, then slunk back to his tent, cold, bruised, and exhausted. He found a vodka-filled water bottle in his pack and drank from it, cinched his sleeping bag tight, and fell asleep.

***

I guess last night wasn't my brightest moment, Stoli thought as he searched for more water. *I should've woken her. That would've been better. Then she would've known it was me giving her all that pleasure.*

They'll understand when I explain it. Maybe not Gordon, but the rest of them. I'll tag behind till the next resupply stop. Where was it? Vermillion Valley Resort?

He gave up looking for water and returned to pack his tent.

Yeah. VVR. Things'll be fine when we get there. I'll play nice. Help Gordon save face. We're the Sideways Seven, for Christ's sake. We're tight. We'll clear things up.

He headed north on the trail.

Behind him, only one tent remained in the meadow.

CHAPTER 22

Being alone sucks, Stoli thought after an hour of hiking. *Never been out here by myself. Since the first day at Lake Morena, I've always been with the Seven.*

The more he walked, the more slowly his watch moved. As his hangover dissipated, he wished he could race Bud or Bacardi up a mountain.

Early afternoon snow at Muir Pass caused him to slide and slip. He began postholing—falling into the snow up to his knees. Extracting himself required tremendous effort.

Why didn't I keep my dick in my pants last night? No lay is worth this.

He reached the stone hut at the top of the pass, wet, worn out, and lonely. His puffy eyes and cheeks throbbed. His legs were red from cold. Nothing on the PCT seemed half as difficult as enduring the isolation of the trail.

Maybe someone'll come along.

He waited a few minutes, rubbing his legs to keep warm. Then he lost patience.

It's freaky up here. All rocks, no life. I won't wait till VVR to catch up. If I step on it, I'll get to them before they pitch camp for the night. I'll keep my distance from Gordon. He might still be sore. Ecstasy would never hold anything against me for long. Even if Gordon blew everything completely out of proportion. We're the Seven. They don't want to be the Six. And I sure as hell don't want to be the One.

So Stoli increased his pace, jogging down the far side of the pass as it descended gently past Lakes McDermand and Wanda.

***

Breeze trailed him by under an hour.

He'd also woken late, with a pounding head and a stomach feeling like someone had installed a wave machine. Inside his tent he groaned, unable to remember where he was or what had happened. Then it hit him.

Jerry.

He unzipped his shelter and staggered to his feet. The meadow was empty. Breeze sank to his knees.

Last night was so close. I almost had him. But then he ran.

He sat back on his heels and massaged his temples.

Think. What would the Seven have done? Gordon was pissed. They must have left without him.

Drinking last night was a mistake. I was too plastered to concentrate. Must've passed out eventually. Now Jerry's gone.

But god bless the Sierras. We're more than halfway to VVR. He can't get off the trail. The bastard's headed north. All I have to do is catch him.

Catching up with Jerry took Breeze into mid-afternoon. Jerry was younger and stronger. The wet snow near Muir Pass cost Breeze time.

He finally caught sight of him at McClure Meadow.

Right near a fucking ranger station. I can't have some National Park Service grunt come running to his rescue.

Breeze bided his time, maintaining a consistent distance between himself and Jerry, sinking lower into the grass and keeping out of sight.

Half a mile past the ranger station, Breeze sprinted up the trail, cutting corners. Branches slapped him in the face. Pebbles flew behind him. He rounded a bend and saw Jerry standing at the edge of Evolution Creek, hands on hips, looking up and down river.

The idiot can't decide where to ford.

Breeze ran.

"Hey. Jerry."

Jerry turned. Breeze approached, panting.

"Jerry."

"How do you know my name?"

CHAPTER 23

"I know you."

Jerry peered at Breeze's face. "Oh. I remember. You're Freeze. From last night. From the poker game."

Breeze stepped closer. "Not Freeze. Breeze. But who the fuck cares? My real name's Ed Galeano. From Oakland. I owned Stoke's Spokes. The bike shop. Ring any bells?"

"No." Jerry turned back to the creek. "Should it?"

Breeze repositioned himself between Jerry and the water. "No? Then how about Kaylee? Kaylee Clark? Ever hear of her?" His eyes narrowed and searched Jerry's face.

"Nope." Jerry shook his head. "Sorry. I can't help you." He walked farther downstream. "But maybe you can help me. Where do you think is better to cross? Over here, or by those trees?"

Breeze's mouth fell open. "Kaylee's the girl you ran…"

Jerry returned and interrupted him.

"Wait till you see." He tugged Breeze's sleeve like an eager child and pulled him downstream. Breeze yanked his arm away. "Trust me, dude. You're gonna wanna see this." Jerry hurried down the bank and pointed at a large set of rocks across the river. "Check it out. Over there. Got ourselves a thru who thinks she's at a nudist camp."

A woman lay on a ledge in the sun, legs spread, one arm resting on her stomach. Jerry skipped back and pulled Breeze's arm insistently.

"See? Told you."

Breeze jerked from Jerry's grip and shaded his eyes to lessen the glare of the sparkling water.

Who's that? Grace? What's she doing here?

"Okay." Breeze snapped his fingers in Jerry's face. "I see her. But forget her. Your problem is *this* side of the river. Your problem is with *me*."

Jerry removed his pack and dug in the top pocket. He pulled out a cell phone and then sat on the bank, stripping off his shoes and socks.

"You stay here." Jerry adjusted the controls on his phone. "I've got to get a picture of this."

Breeze stared. "What the fuck is your problem, man? I'm telling you to forget her. I've been waiting months to meet up with you. The only thing you've got to do right now is listen."

"Sure, man. We can talk. Just let me get a few good shots. If I get out in the middle I think I can zoom in on her beaver."

Jerry chuckled and waded into the river.

Breeze dropped his pack and splashed in after him.

"Shhhh." Jerry turned toward Breeze, put a

finger to his lips, and pointed at Grace. "We don't want to wake her."

"Listen to me. I said leave her the fuck alone."

"I'm not bothering her. One picture won't hurt. A nice close up. I'll have myself the best Facebook post of the hike."

Jerry edged through the water, holding up the phone.

"You bastard."

"Keep it down, man."

Jerry continued to slink toward Grace.

Breeze overtook him and clapped a hand on his shoulder. "Hey, shit for brains. Drop that fucking phone."

Jerry stared at him.

"But it's for fun. Nobody's going to get hurt."

"Somebody's going to get hurt all right."

"Dude, you don't have to worry about me." Jerry snickered. "I've done stuff worse than this. Nothing ever happens. Trouble never seems to find me."

"The reason for that, asshole, is because it finds other people."

Breeze grabbed for the phone. He missed and knocked into Jerry.

"Hey, watch it." Jerry shoved Breeze. "It almost fell in."

Breeze swatted the phone from Jerry's grip. It arced across the water and plopped into the shallows. Jerry's face reddened.

"What'd you do that for?"

Breeze seized Jerry's t-shirt with both hands and yanked him close. Jerry's eyes widened.

"I told you to leave her alone. But you didn't

listen. Well, you'd better start listening to me. Real fast."

Jerry pulled frantically at Breeze's hands.

"Look, I'm sorry. Can't take any pictures now anyway. So let me go. We'll pretend this never happened, okay?"

Dark veins pulsed in Breeze's neck. He leaned in close.

"This never happened? Nothing ever happened?" Spit flew as he spoke. "You say you're sorry and go on with your fucking life?"

Jerry wiped trailing ends of saliva from his cheeks with trembling fingers. Breeze twisted his fists and wrung the fabric of Jerry's shirt like a wet towel, drawing him even closer. Jerry shrugged pathetically and attempted a smile.

"I don't know what you want me to say, dude. Let me go. I'll disappear. You'll never see me again."

Breeze yanked his shirt. Jerry's nose collided with Breeze's forehead. Jerry howled as blood spouted. Breeze loosened his hold and Jerry wrenched away, stumbling into deeper water, clutching his bleeding nose.

"I dink you boke id, you basdard."

He splashed water on his face and blood flowed freely, staining the river around him.

"Who're you calling a bastard?" Breeze hurled himself at Jerry, a rain of pounding fists showering Jerry's back. "You self-centered prick. Months of searching. You don't even pay attention. You fucking ruined my life. You understand?"

Jerry shielded his head from the onslaught and

plunged through deeper water toward the other side of the creek. Breeze staggered after him, landing punches on his ribs.

"That's for Kaylee. That's for my store. That's for Dell. For my money. For my reputation. My fucking life."

"Sop id. You're crazy. I don know whad you're dalking aboud. I never med you before lasd nighd. You've god de wrong guy."

"Like hell."

Breeze clutched Jerry's pants at the waist and lugged him backward. Suddenly, Jerry turned on Breeze with the fury of a cornered animal. He flailed blindly, pummeling Breeze's face and head. Breeze defended himself with raised forearms. The current surged around their legs, threatening to knock them over.

Breeze latched onto Jerry's right arm and in one movement yanked it under the water. The open palm of his free hand shot up and collided with Jerry's chin. Molars smashed together with a crunch. Jerry's head jerked backward. He teetered. Then fell backward.

Breeze heaved himself forward. His knee connected with Jerry's solar plexus. Jerry groaned and tried to regain his legs. Breeze latched onto Jerry's hair with both hands. He scowled into Jerry's puffy, blood-stained face.

"You think you can do anything. Don't you?"

Jerry shook his head.

"Yes, you do. Anything you fucking want."

"No. Plead, no."

"Yes, you do. But I'll fucking show you."

He plunged Jerry's head under the water.

Fingers clawed at his wrists. Jerry's torso twisted. Breeze raised his arms. Jerry coughed and gasped.

"You still think you're king?" Breeze shook him violently. "Answer me."

Panic-stricken eyes stared back at him. Jerry tried to pry Breeze's fingers from his hair.

"You trying to tell me what to do?" Breeze spat in his face. Jerry moaned. "You make me sick." Breeze plunged his head back under the water.

Water splashed in Breeze's face as Jerry squirmed. Legs kicked. Hands tore at his arms. Bubbles rose around them.

Jerry's arms slackened. Dropped to his side. Sank.

Breeze let go. The body bobbed in the undulating current, drifting face down in the direction of the waterfalls.

Breeze dragged himself to the bank. He gazed unseeingly downriver.

The bastard's gone. Serves him fucking right.

Minutes passed. Water on his bare legs and arms shone in the bright light. He rubbed his eyes and scanned the horizon.

No one.

He spat.

Well, Jerry said he wanted to disappear. So I helped him. Gone without a trace.

Then his eyes widened. They swiveled abruptly to the ledge where Grace had been sunning herself.

It was empty.

CHAPTER 24

Shouts woke Grace from her nap on the rock.

Thrus?

She stretched her arms to the bright blue sky.

Where's my tent?

She looked around.

Oh. The river. My phone.

The yelling continued. Grace shaded her eyes from the late afternoon sun and took in the opposite shore, where two backpackers waded into the river.

What are they up to?

She sat and raised an arm to wave, catching as she did so the sight of her bare body.

I'm naked. I'll be the laughing stock of the PCT.

She snatched her warm shirt from the stone and stepped into her shorts. She slipped the components of her phone into its baggie.

I'll fix it later. Hope it works.

As she packed the remainder of her things, the yelling behind her increased in intensity. She stopped to look.

About thirty feet upstream, the two men stood in

the middle of the river. Water surged around their waists.

Is that Stoli and Breeze? What a strange combination.

Stoli started to run.

Well, if he falls in, Breeze will have to help him. See...he's...

Grace leaned forward.

What the heck?

Grace watched Breeze pummel Stoli with blows. Stoli tried to escape. Grace reached her hands toward the figures, as if she could pry them apart. Then Stoli turned on Breeze. They fought savagely.

This is crazy. What's gotten into them?

Grace pulled on her socks. She stowed her camp shoes with her sleeping bag, shoved her feet into her hiking shoes, and clambered off the rock, dragging her pack with her. All the while, she never took her eyes off the scene unfolding before her.

Their voices didn't carry anymore above the churning river. But she saw them attack each other with fury, bodies bent, arms thrashing.

Why don't they stop?

One hand wound tightly around her pack strap, ready to hoist it. She wiggled the toes of her shoes into the dirt, ready to run.

Stoli doubled over under the unrelenting assault. He stumbled, and Breeze latched on. Grace covered her eyes with her free hand. But she peered through the gaps between her fingers, her arms and legs tingling with fear.

I shouldn't be seeing this. I should try to stop them. If Lone Star were here, he'd stop them.

Stoli fell backward in response to a solid blow to his chin and landed with a splash. He struggled to keep his head above water. Breeze flew at him.

"No!" Grace dropped her pack and dashed toward them.

Breeze grabbed Stoli's hair.

Grace turned back toward the ledge. She scooped up her pack and flung it onto her shoulders as she charged down the trail away from the river. At the first corner she paused. Breeze was bent over, arms stiff, holding something under the water.

Grace sprinted faster than any thru she'd met.

Did Breeze see me?

The thought whipped her legs into further action.

He was crazed. Probably blind to everyone but Stoli. But...

Her feet pounded down steep switchbacks toward the South Fork San Joaquin River. Then she reached the canyon floor and slowed her pace at a set of trailside campsites. All the spots were empty.

Where are all the thrus when I need them? Where's my Texas thru? I can't even call him.

Grace skidded to a stop.

Or can I?

She turned back and cupped her hands to her ears.

Breeze isn't on me yet.

She put down her pack. Her fingers groped inside and drew out the phone in its baggie. Her hands shook as she unzipped it. She removed the back cover and replaced the SIM card. Her fumbling fingers dropped the battery on the ground.

Perfect.

It was covered with sand. She blew into the crevices and brushed it with her shirt. The battery slipped into place. She snapped on the cover and pressed the button.

Please work.

She pushed the button again and again. But the phone remained dead.

Maybe it needs to dry out some more.

Her mind flooded with images of Breeze. She disassembled it quickly and continued jogging down the trail. A stream lapped over rocks. The last calls of birds echoed in the woods. Rays of lingering sunlight spilled between the trees and illuminated Indian paintbrushes, which glowed like hot embers in the increasingly cool air.

Later, shadows dimmed and the fir-lined path before her became tinged with blue as twilight grew. Her pace slowed to a trot.

Maybe what I saw back at the river wasn't as bad as I thought? Maybe Breeze wasn't holding him under? Maybe Stoli's okay?

The knot in her stomach loosened. She imagined catching up to some friendly thrus. But half a mile later, she heard from behind the unmistakable thump of someone running.

She raced on as fast as her short legs could manage.

CHAPTER 25

She's gone.

Breeze stared at the empty rock.

She was there when we walked into the river.

He racked his brain for images of Grace after the fight began. But he only called up pictures of Jerry.

Did she see us? There was a lot of yelling. Was she still there at the end?

His stiffened legs protested when he stood.

Only one direction. To Vermillion Valley Resort. Twenty miles. Another day and a half. If Grace saw what happened, she'll be heading there, right to the police. Or the next place she can get cell phone reception to call.

He started down the trail, then stopped.

My pack. It's on the other side.

His eyes flashed across the water's surface, searching for signs of Jerry's body.

Must have gone over the falls.

Breeze plunged in. The icy coldness sucked the warmth from his legs like a vacuum. He fought against the current. At the other side, he hoisted his pack onto one shoulder. As he did, Jerry's pack, shoes, and socks caught his eye.

He flung shoes and socks into the river and slung Jerry's pack over his other shoulder, where it bounced uncomfortably against his torso. Mid-river, he tossed it as far from him as he could. It floated for a few seconds and then submerged.

On the far bank, his wet boots squished.

They'll dry out as I go.

He cinched his waistbelt and shoulder straps and took off.

When I catch up with her, I'll play it cool. If she saw me, I'll know it. We can stay together. If someone sees us, we can pretend we've hooked up. Get to VVR. Then to Fresno. Maybe Canada.

He increased his pace. The trail switchbacked steeply toward the floor of the canyon. He cursed the rocks and widened his stride.

Got to get her before she gets close to a cell tower.

He cut corners, plunging straight down the incline, concentrating on the ground ahead of him, skidding and sliding as stones shifted under his feet, remaining erect only by hurtling headlong down the steep grade.

At the bottom, he followed the trail upstream.

Where the hell is she?

There. That must be her.

He slowed.

Don't want to scare her.

His eyes focused on a yellow tent pitched at a campsite near the trail.

No pack. No shoes. Probably took everything

inside, hoping I won't recognize anything.

Breeze approached slowly across the carpet of fir needles, stopping frequently to listen and look around. He edged closer, picking carefully around twigs and stones. Five feet from the tent, he paused.

Act casual.

He moved in front of the flap. "Hey, Grace. Thought I recognized your tent."

The walls fluttered. Breeze dangled his arms and forced a grin.

Easy now. Don't frighten her.

The zipper lowered. A hand emerged that could have been from a lumberjack axe advertisement, with fingers the size of hot dogs and dark hair sprouting from the knuckles.

"You've got the wrong tent."

A face appeared through the opening. Long, unwashed black hair framed a broad face where a disheveled beard crawled up to two steely blue eyes. They peered at Breeze from above a nose that evidenced a history of breaks.

Breeze stared.

"Man, I thought…your tent looked like…I mean, I was looking for…" Breeze waved both hands apologetically. "Go back to sleep and forget it."

"Sure thing." The man withdrew. The zipper closed. Breeze stood alone.

What was I thinking? Why would that be her tent? How much time did I just waste?

He jogged back to the trail. In the quickly fading light he sprinted ahead, stopping only when he reached a junction with a side trail.

Would she take it to throw me off? Is she waiting

until I pass?

He scanned the branch trail with a calculating eye.

No. She'll stick to the PCT. That's what she knows.

He continued running.

CHAPTER 26

Grace pushed harder. The person behind her was gaining.

Wooden bridge planks clattered as she roared across the stream. She reached the middle and started as the boards rattled to the beat of a second set of footsteps. Grace glanced over her shoulder.

Breeze.

He lunged and grabbed her pack.

She jerked to a stop. "Let me go."

He held on tight. She undid her waist belt. Before she could drop her pack, he yanked her against the rails. Large hands pinned her wrists. Long legs straddled hers.

Their eyes locked. Breeze's cuts and bruises hovered at the edge of her peripheral vision.

He killed him.

Grace's legs trembled. Her hands clutched a rail. She looked beyond Breeze at the rushing water of the creek.

"Why were you running?" Breeze's breath smelled of old alcohol.

She turned her head away. "I could ask you the same question."

"I saw you and wanted to catch up. Kind of like that first time we met. Remember? When you took that tumble down the mountain?"

The cool evening air caught in Grace's lungs. "I remember."

"Good." Breeze released her hands. The wooden slats of the bridge creaked as he took a step back. "I wanted to see if you want to hike together for a bit. Like we used to."

Grace scrutinized his face.

He's lying.

"I'd rather hike by myself. Like you used to. And, anyway, I've got some friends up ahead. They'll come back if I don't catch up soon."

She pushed off and started for the far end of the bridge.

Breeze siezed her wrist. The touch of his fingers made her shudder. She tried to disengage. He held on tighter.

"Okay, look. I don't know what you saw back there at the river. But it wasn't what you think."

Her head tilted defiantly upward. "So what was it?"

Breeze tugged her closer. She resisted by dragging her feet along the planks. He shot her a look.

"Help…" His free hand clamped over her mouth. She tried to bite his fingers but her teeth couldn't gain leverage. With an arm around her neck, Breeze dragged her off the bridge and into a recess behind some adjacent boulders. He forced her back against the stone.

"Don't get any ideas. You don't have any friends out there. Now, what did you see out there by the river?"

She squared her shoulders. "I saw you holding Stoli under the water. And I'm not the only one who knows. I called the police. I told them what I saw. They're coming to get you."

He nodded toward her pack. "So give me your cell phone. Let me look at the calls you made. Put down your pack. Then reach inside and hand it over."

Grace lowered her pack. She dug through it slowly.

What do I have that's sharp?

Her fingers roamed through the contents.

Tent stakes? But they're at the bottom, in a stuff sack.

Kenji's key felt cool against her skin. It was fastened to her first aid kit. She quickly undid the twist tie, palmed the key, and pulled out the baggie with the phone.

Breeze laughed when he saw the disassembled parts. "You didn't call with that thing."

"I tried."

"Uh huh. But I'm guessing you didn't get far. No California state patrol after all." He leaned forward. "So let me tell you what's going to happen. You and I will hike to VVR. On the way, we're going to play boyfriend and girlfriend."

"Never."

Breeze yanked her arm. "Shut up and listen. We're going to *pretend*. That's all. In case we meet anybody. Now, see this?" Breeze drew a five-inch survival knife from the waist belt of his pack. "If you say one word, or if you even hint at anything, I'll use it. And don't play the hero. I won't go after you. I'll hurt anybody you try to tell."

The blood drained from Grace's face.

Breeze leered. "I see you understand."

"What's the plan when we get to VVR?"

"We catch a ride with a nice stranger who wants to help a young couple get to Fresno. Then you rent a car for us."

"And then?"

"None of your business."

Grace looked at the dusty ground. "So is it my business why you killed him?"

Breeze's eyes darkened. "You think I killed Jerry?"

"Who's Jerry?"

"Stoli. Jerry Kriebel. They guy at the river. You're saying I killed him? Well, maybe I did. I'm not saying I did." His eyes bounced erratically from her to the rocks around them. "But *if* I did, that bastard had it coming. Someday, if you get back to San Francisco, look up a bicycle accident. Last year on Mount Tam. On May seventh. It's all over the Internet. Little girl run off the road. He ran her over, and then he ran away from the police. He ran all the way to fucking LA."

Breeze's eyes flicked back and forth. His grip on Grace's arm slackened. She kept her gaze on him but braced her feet, ready to run.

"So what happened to me? My son of a bitch mechanic posts all over the Web, says I'm the one who ran her down. The police believe it, and so do all my customers. My bike shop was the best in Oakland. Six months later it was a ghost town. I lost everything. Meanwhile, Jerry's in LA getting wasted." Breeze's eyes clouded completely. His face wore a haunted expression. He dropped Grace's hand to scratch his forehead.

Grace pushed past him and charged up the trail, screaming for help.

Breeze tore after her and caught the back of her shirt. He wrenched. She turned. The key flashed between her fingers, a jagged point jutting at her assailant. She aimed for his face. And punched.

He blocked it and smacked the side of her head with a backhanded blow, opening a cut above her temple. She fell forward and the key bounced into the brush.

Breeze pulled her back toward the recess. She relaxed her body, willing its dead weight to slow him down, but the rocky surface provided no grip. Branches cut her hands as she grabbed passing tree limbs.

"Bitch." He whipped his knife from its sheath and waved the blade, his face red and distorted with fury. "You try that again and *you're* the one who's going to feel it. If anyone hears you scream, I'll take them out too. No more goddamn loose ends."

Grace felt suddenly nauseous.

I can't let him get to me. Or I'll never get away. I'll take another chance if he gives me one. In the meantime, I can't let him beat me down.

Breeze gestured with his knife to Grace's pack. She put it on. Sweat ran down her brow and she wiped it. Her hand came away red.

"Hey. Don't you think that whole boyfriend-girlfriend routine will look suspicious if I'm bleeding like an amputee?"

Breeze focused on the blood. "What do you want me to do about it?"

"Funny. You caused it. Seems like you should know what to do."

"I'm no medic."

Grace sighed, deposited her pack, and loosened a small hiker towel from the compression straps. She applied pressure to the wound, but each time she removed the towel, the bleeding started again.

He waved the knife near her throat. "We don't have time for this."

"Give me a minute." Grace ignored the threat and explored her pack, resurfacing with her first aid kit.

"Let me see that." She handed him the package.

"Open your hands."

"I'm not palming anything."

He threw the kit back at her. She rubbed an iodine pad over the cut and held a piece of gauze to her head. "You'll have to help. Hold this in place. I'll put on the tape."

He offered one hand but kept the other on his knife hilt. When she finished, she regarded him carefully. He was breathing heavily.

If I get away, it'll be because I outsmart him. A level head's the one thing he hasn't got.

She stepped from their hiding place. Breeze followed. They both scanned the area. The trail was empty.

Grace's hiking poles lay where she'd dropped them on the bridge, one against the bottom railing, the other hanging by its strap over the water. She picked them up and started to wrap the straps around her wrists, but Breeze snatched them from her.

"I'll take those." He loosened the joints, collapsed the poles, and stuffed them into his pack. "Get going. And don't get any ideas. I call the shots."

CHAPTER 27

The night was clear. A brilliant full moon competed with sparkling stars. A smile almost broke through Grace's scared expression when she glanced up.

Hikers out here are looking at the same sky. I only have to find them.

She skidded on some rocks. "Hey. That's about the fifth time I almost fell. Will you finally let me get my headlamp out? I could break something out here."

"Fine. I'll get it out if it will speed you up. We'll never get to VVR at this rate. Turn around."

"It's on top."

He pulled it out and handed it to her. "Turn it on. Then I'll see who's coming. Don't do anything stupid."

They followed the river, hiking past Aspen Meadow and into the tall firs beyond. Grace listened to the crunch of her footsteps on the sandy path and the clomping of Breeze's large boots behind her. She swung her headlamp back and forth

231

and scanned the trail ahead for hikers. Trunks of trees and low hanging branches created a tunnel of light. Grace slowed.

A hiker?

Breeze saw the figure too and took her hand. She jerked it away before thinking. He jabbed the knife hilt into her ribs and reclaimed her hand.

"Easy there, honey. Don't want anyone to get hurt. We're just a pair of lovers out for a midnight stroll. The less said, the better."

Grace nodded. She took off her headlamp and pointed it toward the river as a figure approached.

"Hi there." A young man fidgeted with his hiking poles, poking them nervously into the ground. "Thanks for not blinding me. Are you two heading to Canada?"

"That's our goal." Breeze held up Grace's hand like a trophy. "We're going to make it together or not at all, right, honey?"

Grace nodded. "Right. How about you?"

The youth shrugged his narrow shoulders and fiddled with his pack straps. "Section hiking the John Muir Trail. The campsites aren't much farther, right?" He looked to Breeze.

He's a newbie, Grace thought. *He's scared. But he'd feel even worse if he knew whose advice he was asking.*

"Not far." Breeze pointed. "There's a bunch up the trail."

"Thanks. I probably sound like a wimp. But I hate hiking alone, especially in the dark."

"You don't have a headlamp?" Grace's eyes contracted.

"No." He stood more erect but looked as though the effort depleted him. "I wasn't planning on hiking at night. It took longer than I thought to get this far."

Grace laid a hand on Breeze's arm. She forced her voice up an octave. "Why don't we give him our headlamp, darling? We can always buy another at VVR. We don't need it. The moon's so bright."

"I couldn't take your only light. You must need it. I'll be fine." But his voice quavered.

Grace saw anger sparkle in Breeze's eyes. She forged ahead.

"Sweetie, you know we hardly use it. And you're always saying how you love the moonlight." She held out the lamp to the youth.

"We might need it later." Breeze tried to snatch it back.

Grace moved it out of his reach. "Now, dear, you don't want to cause a scene. It's only a headlamp. This guy is going to remember you forever if you don't give it to him now." She pressed the light into the young man's outstretched hands.

The hiker looked from her to Breeze and back again. "If you're sure."

Breeze nodded slowly.

The man strapped the light to his forehead. "I appreciate this." He hurried off the way Breeze and Grace had come.

They watched his bouncing light until he was out of earshot. Then Breeze rounded on her, his face glowing even in the sparse light. "What the fuck do you think you're playing at?" He shook her shoulders. "What was all that? Why'd you make me give him the light?"

"I thought he might tag along with us if I didn't."

"Why would he come with us? He's going the *opposite* direction, for Christ's sake."

"Because I could see it in his face. He was scared. He wanted company." She held her index finger and thumb an inch apart. "He was *this* close to asking us if he could hike with us. The only way to get him to leave was to give him something to take away his fear."

Breeze's face registered indecision.

He doesn't know whether to believe me or punch me.

After a few moments, Breeze dropped his eyes. "Don't do anything like that again. From now on, I do all the talking."

Grace nodded.

His voice sounds strained. If I can keep him off balance, I might have a chance.

They continued north, Breeze close on Grace's heels. But minute by minute, she heard the rhythm of his footsteps change. Before, his boots pounded behind her with a regular *clomp, clomp*. Now he increasingly favored one foot over the other, *clomp, thud, clomp, thud*. After half an hour, he told her to stop.

"My feet are killing me. Especially the left one. I think I have blisters."

They stood before the steel bridge over Piute Creek. Breeze gestured to some rocks. Grace sat beside him while he removed his boots.

"I wish I had a fucking headlamp." He glowered at Grace, who repressed a smile. He lit a match. The flash revealed two large blisters on the heel of his right foot. His left heel sported a trio of thumb-size, fluid-filled sacks. "Do you have any moleskin?"

"Not much. I don't get blisters anymore. I have a little for emergencies."

"Well, this is a goddamned emergency. Get out what you got. And don't think of doing anything stupid. You won't get far. I can run faster in bare feet than I can in these lousy boots." He looked at Grace and reconsidered. "As a matter of fact, take off your shoes and give them to me. Just to be sure."

Grace pulled off her shoes and handed them to him. "What else do you want? My shirt?"

Breeze grunted. He sterilized the tip of his knife with matches and, with one eye on Grace, burned himself twice. Then he popped the blisters and applied the shreds of her limited moleskin supply.

The night sky glowed with the radiance of the moon. A dense blanket of white stars shone outside its halo.

What about Lone Star? Where is he tonight?

Breeze cocked his head. "There's somebody coming from behind."

Grace listened. Sounds of two pairs of feet walking at a brisk pace drifted toward her. Breeze blew out his match and put his arm around her shoulders. She stiffened. Breeze leaned in.

"Remember, I talk, or those two won't make it out of here."

The headlamps of two hikers lit the path until they stopped in front of them. Grace drew in her breath. One of them was Beartrap.

"How you doing?" Breeze raised a hand in greeting. "Nice night for a stroll."

"Yep." Beartrap's eyes swept quickly over Grace's bandage, Breeze's cuts, and their bare feet. "Everything all right here?"

"My cutie's helping me take care of a couple of blisters." Breeze held up a foot for inspection.

"Looks rough." Beartrap's companion leaned in close. He pulled his auburn hair behind his ears to get a better look. "You want some more moleskin? I have extra."

"I sure could use it." Breeze unwrapped his arm from around Grace.

The second man put down his pack. His arm disappeared and his tanned face assumed an abstracted expression. "You know, there are lots of different kinds of moleskin. Some are better than others."

Breeze peered at him from under a furrowed brow.

The man's hand emerged with a parcel the size of a soda can. "All moleskin. Let me explain what I mean…" Breeze's eyes grew wider as he listened to a dissertation on blister care.

Beartrap winked at Grace.

She glanced at Breeze, who was absorbed in doctoring his foot.

Beartrap raised his eyebrows as if to ask, "Are you really with this guy?"

Grace pressed her lips together and shrugged. "I haven't seen you in a while."

"Yeah. It was Mike's Roadhouse Café in Mojave, wasn't it?"

"Wow. What a memory. I sometimes can't remember the name of my last resupply town."

"Mind's like a steel wastebasket." Beartrap tapped his forehead. "But it's limited to trail things. Off the trail, I can hardly remember my own name."

Grace looked again at Breeze and the other man absorbed in applying multiple moleskin layers.

Grace lowered her voice. "Since you remember trail life, have you ever seen things that weren't what they seemed?"

Beartrap scratched his chin. "I'm not quite sure I get…"

Breeze whipped around. "What kind of stories are you telling this guy, sweetie?" He gave her a kiss on the cheek.

"Nothing, honey." Grace spat out as Breeze turned back to his feet. "So, where are you two headed tonight?"

Beartrap and his friend exchanged looks. "Who knows? Maybe Sallie Keyes Lakes? Maybe farther? It's a great moon for a hike. And we got a late start this morning." He looked at his watch. "Probably keep going for another hour or two, right, Doc?"

"At least that much."

Breeze's eyes narrowed into thin slits. "Why Cop?"

"Not Cop. Doc." He repacked his supplies. "Actually, I'm not a doctor either. Doc's short for Dr. Scholl's. Because I carry a lot of foot care stuff."

"We'd better get going before this guy uses up your whole supply." Beartrap turned to Grace. "Maybe you two will leapfrog us later?"

237

"Maybe."

Grace watched the two men clatter across the bridge. She and Breeze sat in silence. Field mice and ground squirrels gnawed and scratched in the woods behind them. A mother raccoon shooed her family up a tree. An owl hooted. Grace and Breeze didn't move.

Grace forced her features into a smile. "Can I at least filter some water while we're giving them a head start?"

"No. And shut up. I'm thinking."

After thirty minutes, Breeze handed Grace her shoes. They continued north on the trail, Breeze evidencing renewed stamina.

Maybe he won't notice if I speed up a little.

She increased her pace slightly.

Breeze stepped quickly beside her. "I see what you're doing. We're not catching up to them. I set the pace here. Not you."

They climbed the far wall of the canyon. The lonely moon illuminated a steep path with rocks and roots jutting at strange angles. Eerie shadows fell across the trail.

Breeze tripped. "Damn blisters."

Grace suppressed a grin.

An hour later, the trail leveled off. Grace stopped, hands on hips. Her stomach grumbled. "I'm wiped. I haven't eaten since lunch."

"You'll eat when I eat. We're not stopping here. Sallie Keyes Lakes are up ahead. Your friends are probably camped there."

"If I don't eat soon, you'll have to carry me."

"Or kill you. Get going." He kicked her firmly in

the behind.

She moved on, but more slowly.

"You think you're tough." Grace tried to have her voice evidence more courage than she felt. "But if you try anything, I'll scream so loud I'll wake up every hiker within miles."

"Save your breath. Nobody's around. We'll go as far as Selden Pass. Then we can find a place to camp. If we see any tents up ahead, pretend you're a goddamned mouse. Got it?"

"Got it."

At Sallie Keyes Lakes, they passed four tents, each hushed and dark.

Wake up early and come find me.

Grace squeezed her eyes shut for a moment in appeal.

CHAPTER 28

Past the lakes, the PCT climbed out of the forest toward Selden Pass. Only a few straggling, misshapen pine trees found footholds among the ubiquitous grey rock. Patches of snow flecked the landscape. Grace struggled to stay erect.

"Why don't you let me stop and put on my snow spikes?"

"It's a waste of time."

"Fine. I hope you fall and knock yourself unconscious."

"Same to you."

She dug in her heels and proceeded carefully across the slushy ledges. When they neared the top of the pass, Breeze ordered her to stop.

"We can't camp up there." He squinted and pointed to the barren, dark grey ridge outlined in the moonlight. The wind whistled down from the heights and carried on it a hint of frost and subfreezing temperatures to come. He looked around. "I don't want anyone passing us in the night, so we'll leave the trail. Hike cross country till we get to somewhere flat."

Grace scanned the jagged rocks strewn around them. "Where, exactly?"

"Bound to be some place." He pushed her ahead of him. "Up there. You first." He pointed to a grey expanse of boulders and rocks.

"I'm no mountaineer. I can't climb up there."

"You'll figure out a way."

The route was easier than it seemed from afar. But she groaned and complained and made halting progress threading her way across the rock-strewn terrain. Clefts between boulders gaped like dark, menacing mouths ready to swallow an easy meal. After fifteen minutes of climbing, she rounded a corner and emerged onto a terrace. A covering of low grass and small stones shone blue in the moonlight.

"Stop." Breeze assessed the campground. "No one can see us here. Take off your pack. Give it to me. Where's your sleeping bag? At the bottom?"

"I can get it out."

"Yeah. And grab your Swiss army knife or whatever. Then we have ourselves a little problem. No way. I'm in charge of your stuff now."

He dug through her pack, found the stuff sack with her sleeping bag, and threw it in her direction.

Grace caught it. "What about my tent?"

"You don't need it. We'll cowboy camp."

"Cowboy camp? Forget it. You need me till we get to Fresno. You can't let me freeze." She crossed her arms.

"You're not going to freeze."

Grace sensed he wasn't convinced. "I'm sleeping

in my tent. You and I know it's going down around freezing tonight. It's already windy. If we cowboy camp, we'll both get frostbite."

Breeze didn't answer.

"Okay, have it your way." Grace unbuttoned her long-sleeved shirt.

"What the hell are you doing?"

"If you're going to give me hypothermia, you might as well do it right. I'm sleeping in the nude." Grace shivered in the cold breeze and pulled down her shorts.

"Put that stuff back on. You're probably right. It'll be warmer if we sleep in the same tent."

He dug deeper in her pack and pulled out her tent and poles. He dropped them at her feet.

"You won't fit."

Breeze laughed. "You're telling me you never shared your tent with anyone?"

"I won't share it with you." She kicked the tent back at him. "I'd rather freeze to death." She stepped out of her shorts and stood naked. Goose pimples covered her body.

"Oh, what the fuck. I can't deal with your hysterics. You're not going anywhere anyway." He threw her tent back at her. "Set it up over there." He pointed to the middle of the clearing. "Make sure the entrance faces my direction."

Breeze sat on a rock, hands on his thighs, and watched her erect the tent.

Grace cleared the area, kicking aside desiccated bear scat and removing stones. After it was assembled, she flung the sleeping bag inside.

Breeze marched over. "Now get in. And pass me

your shoes."

Grace crawled in and hurled her hiking shoes as far as she could manage. One ricocheted off a tree trunk and shot into the underbrush. The other caught on a low branch and dangled, rotating on its laces.

"Bitch." Breeze retrieved the shoes. "That's going to cost you half a dinner."

Grace huddled in her sleeping bag, waiting. Breeze set up his tent a yard from hers. Then his hand thrust into her tent opening. Grace jumped.

"Dinner." He dropped two chocolate power bars and her San Diego County Parks water bottle onto the nylon floor. The bottle rolled until it collided with her elbow. The hand disappeared. Grace zipped her tent shut. Half an hour later, Breeze returned.

"Hand over the water bottle."

"What? You think it's a weapon?"

"No. I'm not leaving you with any essentials. See how far you get with no water and no shoes."

The unzipped flap let in a cool breeze. Grace slapped the empty bottle into his open hand.

Her tent shook and she peeped outside. Breeze was winding a long, thin rope in complicated loops around both their packs and the guy-lines. When he exhausted the supply of rope, he climbed inside his shelter, one end still in his hand.

She cupped her hands in the direction of his tent. "Hey, I've got to pee."

"Hold it."

"I can't."

"So go pee."

"I can't."

"What? Afraid of bears?"

"No. You have my shoes."

Curses floated on the night air. After a minute, she stuck her head outside and ducked as two shoes whizzed by her ears. Breeze stood a few feet away, scowling in the half-light, bundled in a balaclava and down jacket. Grace retrieved her shoes on tiptoe. He followed close behind as she walked into the shelter of a grove of trees.

"Turn your back while I go."

"Dream on."

Grace pulled down her shorts and squatted. Nothing happened. "I can't do it if you're looking."

"Guess we're gonna be here for a while."

Breeze leaned against a tree and stuck his hands under his armpits. She turned away and concentrated on the moon, its craters visible as grey shadows on the luminescent surface. When she finished, they traipsed back to camp in a whistling wind. Grace crouched and began to crawl inside her tent.

"Where do you think you're going with those shoes?"

Grace flipped over, pulled them off, and handed them to him without comment.

In a moment, his muffled voice penetrated her tent wall. "I've got the end of the rope around my wrist. I'm a light sleeper. If you get up, I'll feel it. My watch is set for four thirty. That means five hours of sleep. If you're fast."

Grace struggled to keep her eyes open. But not even the rocks digging into her back and hips could keep her weary body from shutting down. In less than a minute, she was asleep.

She dreamed a distorted mixture of events. At the end, Stoli's body floated face up in the current of a river. Grace edged closer. Stoli tried to tell her something. Just as she thought she understood, a noise startled her awake.

The yellow ceiling of her tent shook. A great muzzle pressed itself against the wall.

Bear.

Grace lay still, hoping the enormous creature would lose interest.

Go away. Please go away.

After less than a minute of sniffing, the bear lumbered off among the rocks.

Grace listened for its return.

Nothing.

Still not quite awake, she unzipped her tent flap and ran her hand along the ground, searching for her shoes.

Where'd they go?

She tried to remember what she'd done with them. Then awareness of the past hours flooded her thoughts. Her watch showed over an hour before Breeze's alarm went off.

I might be his prisoner, but there's one thing he doesn't know.

She reached into her sleeping bag, drew forth the stuff sack, and shook it. Out plopped her yellow camp shoes.

Celine, thank you.

"One day out there I'm sure you'll appreciate my advice," Celine had said when she added the foam clogs to Grace's enormous pile at the REI checkout counter. "Kenji told me these things can come in handy. And, heck, they don't weigh much."

You were absolutely right. Grace slipped the yellow shoes on her feet. *These come in very handy.*

CHAPTER 29

The moon hung lower in the early morning sky. But it still cast pale shadows as Grace sneaked out of her tent, careful not to disturb the bear rope on the guy-lines. In the dim light, the sight of Breeze's tent and pack sent shivers up her spine.

She held her breath and slinked across the grass. When she reached the edge of their campsite, she stared at the rocky descent that lay between her and the trail and winced.

How can I make it down there without starting an avalanche?

She tread from one rock to another and began threading her way down the slope. She had only traversed a few yards before a loose stone undermined her balance. Her hands clutched a tree branch, but not before rocks clattered down the incline, making a roar she thought would be heard for miles.

Her heart thundered in her ears.

Run for it? Wait?

Run, she decided, and stepped onto another loose

rock. This time she fell, the impact knocking the air from her lungs. Stars stared down at her through branches of a windblown fir.

About to die. Like my first day in the desert. When Lone Star found me.

She closed her eyes and waited for Breeze.

But nothing stirred.

She rose and looked around. No one.

She tried her camp shoes on the side of the nearest boulder.

Maybe if I climb?

Her fingers searched for a crevice as her shoes pressed into the stone. She clambered up and slid across the top on her behind. On the other side, she hopped lightly to the ground. At the next huge rock, she repeated the procedure. Progress was slower, but quiet.

When she'd covered half the distance back to the trail, she judged she was out of earshot and began to jog. Her strides sent tiny rocks showering in all directions.

I've already wasted enough time.

The trail to Selden Pass proved less easy to find than she anticipated. Moonlight made judging distances difficult. False trails petered out and left her more disoriented than before. Finally, she glimpsed the unmistakable sandy thread of the PCT snaking between the rocks like an iridescent python.

On the trail she broke into a run. She hammered up the ascent to the top of Selden Pass. Her ribs heaved and thighs protested. She ignored them.

He's bigger, stronger, and faster. What was it on the map? Five miles of mixed terrain between me and VVR? I'll try and get past the meadow. If he catches up with me in the woods after that, maybe I'll hear him coming and can hide.

On the north side of the pass, the trail fell toward Marie Lake's many rocky islands. Here, her run turned into a gravity-assisted sprint. Without a pack, she felt light and free and flew in gigantic strides. On snowy patches, she slid and swerved on the soles of her camp shoes like a professional skier, arms outstretched for balance, fueled by the adrenaline of panic.

At the edge of the lake, she scooped handfuls of the dark water into her parched mouth, ignoring images of squirming microbes that floated through her mind.

Intestinal upset's the least of my worries.

Ten minutes before Breeze's alarm went off, she reached the meadow.

Grace felt like an exposed antelope in a field of crouching tigers in the grassland. Her grey shirt and tan pants shone as though made of reflectors. She longed for camouflage gear. She imagined Breeze behind trunks and boulders, and her muscles tapped into a secret store of energy she hadn't known she possessed.

The route crossed a bridge. Then the trail entered a lodgepole forest. In a stillness broken only by the rustling of needles in the wind, she heaved a sigh. Little light filtered through the boughs, making the path indistinct. She looked at her watch.

Breeze must be awake. If he catches up with me here, at least I have a place to hide.

Fallen needles muffled her footsteps. She

strained her ears for the sound of anyone approaching, but only the twitter of early rising birds and the whoop of an owl accompanied her.

He can't get here that quickly anyway.

The trail emerged at Bear Creek. She stepped in without hesitation. Frigid water submerged her leg to mid-calf. The current pulled, and she wished she'd chosen a stick before plunging in.

I can't fall. I won't.

She picked her way carefully across, leaning upstream to compensate for the relentless flow. Her camp shoes slid on slimy stones and shifting sand. She concentrated on the opposite bank until she stepped safely onto the shore.

An unmarked junction faced her. An uphill route followed a branch of the creek. The other path sloped gently down the canyon.

Which way's the PCT?

Panic rose in her chest.

VVR's lower than Selden Pass. I haven't lost much altitude so far. So it must be downhill.

She crossed her fingers and jogged through the dark woods, pushing out of her mind the thought that the PCT often went up before it went down.

Forty-five minutes later, a suffusion of brilliant blue, yellow, and orange lit the sky in the east as the sun pushed away the curtain of night. Grace slogged up the winding trail toward the crest of Bear Ridge. Lake Edison and VVR lay at the bottom of a long set of switchbacks beyond the crest.

Almost three hours since I left.

Her feet dragged as she plodded along the trail that wound among the ubiquitous grey boulders.

Her stomach had long forgotten the two power bars from the night before. Increasingly demanding thoughts of food pestered her.

I wish I had a chocolate bar with nuts and raisins. That last cup at Kennedy Meadows, half coffee, half cream, and three teaspoons of sugar. The pepperoni and mushroom pizza Lone Star and I shared, shining with oil and extra cheese that stretched into thin strings when I pulled out a slice.

Ow.

A misstep shot pain up her leg, interrupting her reverie. The exertion of the climb sliced into her calves and thighs. She felt faint. Her knees shook.

He can't be far behind me now.

But the image of Breeze didn't prompt the adrenaline rush it had before. She recommenced the ascent with weary steps. Her eyes focused only on the next turn in the trail.

Her dragging foot caught on a rock. She tumbled, and her left knee collided with a stone on the way to the ground. When she flexed the limb, strong waves of nausea accompanied the pain. She sat in the dirt, leg stretched before her, waiting for the queasiness to subside.

I'm almost at the top. After that it's all downhill to VVR. I have to keep going.

But her body fought the thought.

Then a flash of light glinted through the trees below. She sprang to her feet, the pain forgotten. Her eyes squinted.

What was that?

She saw it again.

Oh my god.

Something dangling from Breeze's belt reflected the early morning light. His knife.

CHAPTER 30

Grace's feet tore at the dirt as she scrambled up the switchbacks. She cut corners across rocky terrain, using her hands to scrabble across loose stones. Dirt and gravel sailed behind her. Her feet struggled for footholds. Her muscles strained with each fresh exertion.

She didn't dare waste time looking back. In her mind, Breeze was close on her heels, though the noise of her own ascent drowned out any other sound. Snagging twigs felt like hands. The wind like his breath. The clutching in her throat like his fingers closing around it. The crest of the ridge felt as far away as it had been when she first noticed him.

Faster.

Near the top, the trail leveled. Grace flung herself over the last incline, onto the dusty path, and hazarded a glimpse over her shoulder. Breeze had halved the distance between them. He clambered straight up the canyon wall like a mountain lion.

Grace raced across the short crest against the

objections of her body. Her clogs felt like magnetized moon boots. Her arms swung as though through wet cement. A corset encased her lungs.

Faster.

The descending trail rapidly metamorphosed into a foot-wide gravel lane wedged between pine trees, rocks, and boulders. It zigzagged down the steeply sloping incline, turning back on itself every two-hundred feet. Grace gave up cutting corners.

Too steep.

She kept to the path and sprinted. Her yellow shoes pounded the trail. Smaller rocks skidded from beneath her. The sound of scattering stones from above warned her that Breeze was narrowing the gap.

Faster.

A rumble overtook her. A surge of debris showered the trail, cascaded down the mountain, and echoed across the canyon wall. Grace looked up. Breeze was cutting switchbacks. Hurtling down the slope from tree to tree. Dislodging large stones as he ran. He crashed, arms outstretched, into a trunk. Then pointed himself at the next tree and took off again.

No.

She mimicked him and chose a tree below, plunging down the incline, feet slithering on the shale. The trunk broke her fall, but the stump of a broken branch dug fiercely into her shoulder. She pushed off immediately and raced toward another tree farther down.

But there were fifty-seven switchbacks leading down from Bear Ridge.

Breeze steadily reduced the distance between them.

Grace's world contracted to one tree at a time. On reaching it without falling. On flinging herself toward the next.

Faster.

She heard him only a few trees behind. The air vibrated with the clatter of displaced stones and cascading gravel. At the next tree, she felt a rush of wind. Out of the corner of her eye she saw Breeze arrive a second too late to grab her arm.

Faster.

She ricocheted off the next tree without stopping. And plummeted downhill.

Faster.

Footsteps hammered the ground.

Get away.

She spun and charged sideways across the slope instead of down.

Breeze hurtled past her. He skidded to a stop at a tree below.

Grace stood panting. Breeze was already ascending the slope. She scratched her way up the stones, weaving back and forth to scatter debris in his face. But the uphill climb advantaged Breeze's leg length and strength.

He lurched forward and grabbed at her ankle. She kicked dirt and pebbles. A rock hit his face with a crunch. He spat out a curse, then renewed his charge up the hillside. Another few seconds and his hands tightened around her waist.

Grace fell with his pull instead of resisting. They both sailed into the air, tumbled down the slope, bounced over stones and roots, and crashed through the underbrush.

Dirt and sticks flew. Breeze released his hold.

She heard him yell.

She flipped onto her stomach and dug her hands and feet into the ground until she stopped and lay motionless, bruised and bleeding, her face pressed against the hard soil. After a minute, she caught her breath and clambered to her hands and knees. She scanned the hill below with frightened eyes.

He's gone.

Grace grimaced. The pain was so ubiquitous that she couldn't pinpoint its source. A few feet above lay the trail. She regained it with difficulty and surveyed the still empty slope.

Where is he?

She hobbled down the incline.

Get to VVR.

She held her right arm to protect her aching shoulder and the strangely twisted wrist that she could no longer move. Squeaks of ground squirrels made her jump. Her eyes swiveled constantly. Back and forth across the trail. Up the mountainside. Behind. She scanned trees, boulders, and bushes, but no one erupted from the shadows.

Twenty minutes later, the forest thickened. Pine trees crowded close upon the narrow path. Her head spun with pain and fatigue.

I can't make it.

Then a roar exploded from among the trees.

Breeze leapt and knocked her to the ground. Grace screamed as her injured arm collided with a rock.

He landed on top of her and straddled her torso. His hands latched around her throat. Fingers crushed her windpipe. Her neck twisted and arched back over a rock.

She gazed up at the leering face distorted by pine needles stuck to matted blood. One eye bulged with hatred. The other was swollen shut.

Grace closed her eyes.

Breeze's voice was unrecognizable. "This time. You're not. Getting away."

Grace opened her eyes.

I'm. Still. Fighting.

She glimpsed bone glinting through a ragged gash in Breeze's forearm. Grace's good hand aimed and punched the bruised and bloody skin. Breeze howled with pain and released his grip.

"Fucking bitch."

Grace tried to roll over. But he pinned her body more tightly between his knees. She twisted and grabbed for his shirt. He leaned away, squeezing her ribs.

Then she watched him lift his knife, holding it between open palms. He raised it over her head.

Her scream echoed down the mountain.

She averted her eyes in the final instant before a bright flash and a seemingly never-ending blackness enveloped her.

CHAPTER 31

"Grace." It was a man's voice. "Grace, darlin', wake up."

I don't want to.

Grace's eyes fluttered despite herself. Shadows of faces surrounded her.

Mom. Dad. Hope. Celine.

"Lone Star? Is that you?"

"Yep." His Texas drawl elongated the word into two syllables. "Glad to see you've decided to join us."

Her heart skipped a beat.

"Where am I? What are you doing here?"

She focused for the first time on the white walls and had a vague impression of a clear plastic bag on a hook next to the bed. "I'm in a hospital?"

"Right again."

The crowd thronged her, clogging her ears with words of congratulation and questions about how she felt. The room spun.

A woman in green scrubs appeared. "Give her a while."

The next time Grace opened her eyes, only Celine sat by her bed.

Celine smiled. "You're awake."

Grace shifted on the pillow. "What happened?"

Celine wrinkled her brow. "You're probably not ready for a long story. Maybe I'd better get a nurse."

"No. I'm okay. I want to know."

Celine's eyes flicked from Grace to the call button and back. "What do you remember?"

Grace's mind floated on a sea of unwelcome memories. Celine half rose from her chair before Grace held her arm.

"It's all right. Give me a second. The last thing I remember…" She paused and forced calmness into her voice. "I saw someone get murdered. I need to talk to the police."

Celine nodded. "We know. The police know. They've been out there already. They found Jerry Kriebel's body in the river."

"You mean Stoli? A tall, young guy with brown hair?"

"I certainly hope there was only one body floating in the river." Celine's attempted laugh emerged as only a long exhalation. "Some hiker found it. There were police at Vermillion Valley Resort before we even got on the trail."

"You were on the PCT? Who's we?"

Celine edged the white plastic chair closer to the side of the bed. "Let me start from the beginning." Her eyes gazed at a corner of the room. "A few weeks ago this guy started calling your office."

Grace raised her eyebrows. "What guy?"

259

Celine laid fingers to her lips. "Hush. Let me tell the story. He was pretty persistent. But they wouldn't give out any information. So, eventually, he found me. Got any ideas which hiker dude was trying to get in touch with you?"

Grace grinned. "Lone Star."

"Well, kinda. Lone Star to you. Gus to me. Gus and I got to be real buddies. He felt horrible about not being able to contact you after he got hurt. He was worried you'd think he'd forgotten you. I think you know the rest."

"He came to meet me."

"Yeah. And after that he and I cooked up a plan. We met here in Fresno and drove to VVR. We hiked up the trail to surprise you as you came down."

"So you were there when Breeze tried to…"

Celine looked down at the covers. "I was there. So was Gus. He's the one who saved you."

"Saved me?"

"We heard screams. Gus recognized your voice. He took off like a cheetah. I've never seen anyone move so fast. I couldn't keep up, but I kept him in sight. He saw that guy about to…so Gus came up from behind and kicked that knife like a football. It flew straight into a tree. And the guy…"

Grace nodded for her to continue.

"He got up. Gus rushed him. The guy was totally crazed. Fought like a madman and ripped away. Ran straight down the hill, right at me. Lost his balance. And, girl, I tell you, he fell. Rolled like he was made of rubber. Legs and arms all over the place." Celine shivered. "I can't get that image out of my head. He practically landed at my feet. Awful. Worst thing I've ever seen." She squeezed her eyes shut.

Grace reached out her hand. "I'm so lucky you were there."

"I didn't do anything." Celine squeezed Grace's fingers. "Gus's the one who did all the work. He broke his arm in the fight."

A man pushed open the door. "You did plenty, Celine. Don't let her tell you no different, Just Grace, honey. It was Celine's cool head that got you to a hospital."

Lone Star strode into the room and winked at Celine. His suntanned face and light pink shirt peeked out from behind an enormous bouquet of red roses. He deposited the cut crystal vase on a bedside table with one arm and leaned over.

Grace's awareness contracted to the soft touch of skin against skin, to the caress of his hand as it cupped her face. She closed her eyes as their lips met and opened them to see the loving gaze of his blue eyes that told her all she wanted to know. Her lips broadened into a smile that beamed both passion and contentment.

"On the trail they told me to be happy where I was." She snuggled into his arm. "Lone Star, my love, I am happy."

Celine tiptoed out of the room.

Later, Grace gazed out the hospital window at towering Sierra peaks shrouded in morning haze. Lone Star followed her glance as he sat at her bedside, his uninjured hand engulfing hers. "You'll get back to the trail someday."

"We'll get back when we're ready." Grace locked her eyes with his. "But next time you're walking slowly. Because look what happened when you let me out of your sight."

"Don't worry. I'm not letting you out of my sight again."

***

Two weeks later, Celine and Grace sat cross-legged on the floor of Grace's dining room. The carpet was littered with unsent resupply boxes, hiking gear, empty plastic bins, and baggies of food. Vases of red roses crowded the remaining space. Grace gazed past the detritus and out the window at the twinkling San Rafael Bay twilight. Her back rested against an overflowing cardboard box.

Celine sat opposite, beer bottle in hand. She gestured with a huge grin at the box Grace leaned against. "So, when's Mr. Teleflora arriving?"

"Tomorrow." Grace's eyes shone with joy. "He's taking the morning flight from El Paso. We're using the long weekend to hike in Marin."

"Flying must be less expensive than sending you flowers. And probably better for the environment. For a guy who loves nature, he's not very eco-conscious."

"I think it's sweet." Grace's mouth crinkled at the corners. "He said he'd send a bouquet for every day he wasn't with me on the trail."

"Ugh. Way too romantic. Do I still have time to buy stock in the floral delivery company?"

"He's still got a few weeks left to send them."

"I'll tell my broker."

They laughed. Celine reached into the box behind Grace and pulled out a size fourteen hiking shoe. "He left his stuff here, I see. Smart guy. Since he's half living here already." She rummaged through more of the contents and held up a nylon sack. "You got a new tent. A two person model?"

"I tossed my tent in the hospital dumpster before Mom and Dad picked me up. Too many memories. Especially with Breeze being dead." She shuddered.

Celine let the new tent drop. "That fall he took. Still gives me nightmares." The two of them stared at the lights in the bay. "Speaking of your parents, you know they were off the charts worried about you, right? Your mom even called me when she heard. She said they'd take their house off the market if you didn't get better."

"I don't believe that for a second. Those two are so excited to be moving to Atlanta. Hope needs them. Anyway, I'm fine. The cast comes off in three weeks." She waved an orange plastered arm.

Celine shrugged. "I'm pumped you're on the mend. But a normal person would consider themselves in the recovery phase. You and Gus are both still in casts. Hiking with your arm in a sling. That's hardcore."

"We don't think about it that way." Grace fingered the laces of Gus's hiking boot. "It's strange. I'm back here in my, quote, normal life. But nothing about it seems normal anymore. Cars go too fast. People are all in a rush. Lone Star says I have to get used to transitioning between on and off the trail."

"Maybe things'll be easier in Texas."

"I'm eager to see."

Celine sipped her beer. The two women gazed at the sun's fading pink shadow in the sky. Celine broke the silence. "I'm thinking of going back to school."

"Celine, that's awesome."

"I'm going to be single for a while, so I want to make good money. I figure computer science will start me on the path to becoming a dot com millionaire." Anticipation and mischief sparkled in Celine's eyes.

"You won't be single forever. Not someone as smart and gorgeous as you."

"No." Celine pushed long, thin braids from her forehead with an exaggerated fashion model sweep. "Not forever. But your brother's a hard act to follow."

"Yes, he is. I keep wondering what he would have done if he'd been out there instead of me."

"You mean the murder?"

"I mean all of it. The hike, the storms, the heat, the cold, the blisters, the people. No matter how many times I go over it in my head, in the end, I'm happy it was me. Kenji would have done fine. But I think, despite all my worries and my total lack of preparation, I was the best person to handle it."

"Could be."

"You know what's absolutely crazy?"

"What?"

"Except for the end, the final two days, I wouldn't go back and change any of it. Even if I could. Do I sound like a freak?"

"You mean you'd want to go through the desert and all the mountain climbing and everything?"

"Well…" Grace paused. "It's hard to explain. I started hiking to get away from my life. Instead, I ended up being happy with it the way it is."

"Finding your true love might have something to do with that."

"Moving on. That's what it was. I didn't stay stuck."

"So Gus doesn't get any credit?"

"He gets all the credit. But I'd never have found him if I hadn't left my old life behind."

Grace pushed herself off the floor and pulled Celine up with her good arm. "Want to help me clean up a bit before he comes? Some things are tough with a cast."

They picked their way through boxes and flowers. Grace pushed open the white bedroom door. Celine jerked to a stop, eyes wide.

Bedframe parts reclined against the walls. A queen-size mattress and box spring leaned precariously against a pine dresser. Two sleeping bags rested side by side on the hardwood.

"You took your bed apart because you two want to sleep on the floor?"

Grace winked. "Celine, there's one thing you have to understand." She stepped around the sleeping bags and tossed Celine an empty clothes hamper. "I learned an important lesson out there. I learned you can take a thru out of the wilderness, but you can never take the wilderness out of a thru."

The End

About the Author

Christine Hartmann grew up in Ohio and Delaware and loves traveling to exotic, romantic settings. After a college semester in Kathmandu, her first three "real" jobs were all in northern Japan, where she lived for almost 10 years. She currently splits her career between her daytime occupation (improving the quality of veterans' nursing home care) and her nights/weekend avocation (writing both fiction and non-fiction books). Her husband Ron Strickland is a well-known long-distance hiker, trail guide writer, and the founder of the 1,200-mile Pacific Northwest National Scenic Trail. Christine loves reading, pilates, bicycling, snorkeling, and health foods that taste like they're bad for you. You will often find her at a keyboard, a German shepherd at her side, and Ron whispering sweet edits over her shoulder.

Facebook:
https://www.facebook.com/christine.w.hartmann

Twitter:
https://twitter.com/chartmannbooks

Website:
http://chartmannbooks.com/

Goodreads:
https://www.goodreads.com/chartmannbooks

Made in the USA
Monee, IL
10 June 2026

53029982R00159